The Undergroun

By Dr Charlie Tweed

Copyright 2014, Dr Charles Tweed.

All Rights Reserved. This book or any portion thereof may not be produced or used in any manner whatsoever without the express written permission of the author, except for the use of brief quotations in a review

Preface

The number of medical facts expected to be learnt by medical students and doctors is really quite vast. Much of the physiology, pathology, pharmacology, histology, biochemistry and other subjects involved are so complicated that they leave even the most wise and intelligent of us baffled. And even if they are not baffled- it may take them several episodes of reading and re-reading for the details to finally stick in our hippocampus.

It is in our nature as human beings to attempt to accumulate as much knowledge and detail as quickly as possible. This often amounts to hours upon hours of wrought learning in the same way day in day out. In fact the most effective method would be to vary our learning including the environment we learn in, the material we learn from, and the way in which this material is put across to us. Various memory studies have shown this, yet many of us fail to listen. It can be difficult with the stresses and pressures of deadlines and exams to not bury one's head in a book for hours on end, writing out lists to attempt to cram knowledge into our brains. The reality is that while this works, it is not for the long term.

This book aims to make the learning of medical knowledge slightly less mundane. Numerous times have I sat in a lecture theatre drifting off and day dreaming about what is on the television later in the day, or whether in fact it would be worse to be eaten by a great white shark or a whale. Numerous times have I been stumped- sitting and learning boring fact after boring fact after boring fact.

So I present to you a very different style of medical text book. This book aims to help make some of the key facts required for medical school and beyond stick in your brain, not just for the exam you are to sit and then to forget afterwards, but for good. By putting medical scenarios and facts in the context of a novel, I hope that this book may make you learn and revise things in a way which is a bit more interesting than the usual dull lectures or list based text books.

The book's main focus is emergency scenarios including but not exhaustively: Basic trauma and haemorrhage, MI, stroke, diabetic coma, overdose, meningitis, renal failure as well as some chronic diseases. Often, patient problems are portrayed as one dimensional in order to explore the certain specific condition or complaint. Realistically, there may be many pathologies and factors presenting to a doctor.

This first book of the series covers some of the more general medical and emergency topics. The books which will follow include a second which covers psychiatry, a third obstetrics and gynaecology, a fourth Paediatrics and another in Surgery and its principles.

Despite the fictional scenarios which run through each book and onto the next, every bit of medicine described is correct to real life.

I hope you enjoy reading and find this as useful as I hope it to be.

Chapter One: Iraq, June, 2013.

The Chinook helicopter touched down with a bump and the exit ramp slowly opened, making a whirring sound. A widening beam of bright light shone in from Iraq's harsh sun. Hot, sharp dust hit Ian Mellows in the face. He grimaced and his blue eyes began to water. The dry heat filled in all around him as sweat poured down his face, which the dust stuck to. The sound of the rotary blades was deafening. Captain Jim Reece, the anaesthetist who Ian was being mentored by looked short of breath his body armour was so tight. Maybe he could not help this for he was a broadly framed man. Chins flopped out over the edge of his combat jacket telling his keenness for the mess bar. He smiled at Ian, and Ian smiled back. Ian did not mean to return the gesture of cheer. He was absolutely terrified. For the fourth time in the last five minutes, he opened his desert parka and checked his body armour for his combat application tourniquets and personal morphine supply. He slung his medical bag over his shoulder. He then checked his pistol was cocked, and his shotgun loaded. He prayed to god he would not have to use them again. Then, all at once, hell broke loose.

Eruptions of bangs and pings, thumps and crashes as bullets smashed against the armour plating of the helicopter- it was like being in the drum of a washing machine. Ian tensed and threw himself to the floor. "Ambush!" someone shouted, and the 0.50 Cal. machine gunner fired with a roar like a lion's at targets Ian could not see. Was this it? The helicopter shook violently like it was in an earthquake and Ian's bones resonated. Voices screamed in his ear over the PRR radio. "Man down! Man down!"

The eight man ambush response team belted out of the rear of the helicopter one after the other and Ian watched as rounds of tracer whipped across in front of the exit ramp. Nothing would make him go out there. Not again. His heart raced. His hands trembled. His eyes closed and he covered his head with his hands. He lay there in a blur as chaos engulfed him. Jim, annoyed at his passiveness whacked him hard on the shoulder. His eyes were as red as his face. His dust glasses were covered in sand. "Get up! 2 casualties! We've got to get them in now! Come on!"

"But I'm only a medical student!" Ian said petrified. "It is too dangerous!"

"No, you are a medical operative on Her Majesty's service and people are dying. Now get up!" Jim shouted back.

Ian shook himself as Jim wrenched him up under the arm. He was strong! A bullet smashed the window behind them splintering tiny shards of glass down the back of his neck. Another explosion boomed above the sound of the helicopter.

"Get them in quickly! Multiple targets to front and right flanks," the pilot's voice was quick and agitated. "We won't stay here long!"

Ian's face was pale, his palms sweaty. He fought to steady his shaking hands. Jim manhandled him to his feet. Ian summoned the courage to move his legs. Ian pulling and Jim pushing, they launched down the exit ramp of the Chinook and onto the hot desert soil of Iraq.

They were almost blown over by the downdraft from the helicopter blades. Ian's rib cage beat like a drum from the woosh-woosh-woosh of the pressure waves- he sprinted, zig-zagging this way and that to avoid bullets, shrapnel and everything else that was flying through the air. The helicopter blades still thundered around and around like propellers of the Titanic ramming its iceberg. Ian could not understand how it had not been hit by an RPG yet. A bullet zipped just in front of his face. He ducked. You could smell adrenaline in the air. Jim led Ian towards a soldier who waved frantically from behind a clay hut. In the distance, Ian could see black flags waving.

Throwing themselves behind the building, Ian tripped on a rock and landed on top of Jim in a heap. "Get off!" Jim shouted angrily. That was when Ian saw the casualties. So much blood. Writhing. Mangled. Burnt flesh. Smouldering.

"We have two casualties! Both T1 priority!" The patrol medic shouted at them wide eyed. His body armour and combat jacket were drenched in blood and he was panting desperately for breath.

"Is the area secure?" Jim shouted.

"No idea sir! It's the IED which triggered the ambush so who knows what else is out there- but we've got enough men to guard you while you work, we'll worry about the insurgents so you can evacuate the casualties!" As he spoke Ian panned his vision to the left and spotted a soldier lying away from their cover with most of his neck blown away, sat in a pool of blood. He was horrendously pale, lifeless and still. He had T4 written on his forehead. He was dead. Ian wretched.

Jim slapped him on the helmet with the butt of his pistol. He screamed at him pointing towards a body. "You're going to have to deal with that one on your own or they'll both die! Get on to Dr Merlin on your radio set!" They crouched behind a high mud brick wall which was amongst a cluster of village houses. Soldiers were dotted about the place returning fire towards the enemy- Ian had no idea where they were attacking from. He could tell from the amount of firepower that there were a lot of them. Were they going to be over run? He knew all too well what happened to people they captured. Zip-zip-zip! More tracer rounds flew overhead like fireworks laced with death.

The patrol medic went back to talking to one of the casualties. The soldier's legs were two bloody and mangled stumps, with tourniquets applied around the thighs. He had severe burns to his face and neck. Jim frantically went about keeping him alive. Ian crawled over to the casualty Jim had assigned him. He took a deep breath and tried to clear his mind. "ABCDEs, ABCDEs, ABCDEs," he repeated to himself over and over and over. He completely forgot about the military mnemonic of CABC where you treat the catastrophic haemorrhage first- but this did not matter for the patrol medic had already dealt with it.

He fought to steady himself. "Master your fear," he said to himself. He moved closer. The soldier's foot was hanging off, attached only by a few bits of fascia and muscle- huge chunks of flesh had been blown away from his lower leg. Ian, could see a lot of bone, and fat was attached here and there, burnt and yellow and wrong looking. It was the definition of a mangled limb. A tourniquet was fixed higher up the leg, he could not tell which arteries were hit but the blood loss seemed to be controlled. The man was white as a sheet, reaching towards his mangled foot, like a child confused as to why a most treasured teddy bear had its stuffing pulled out. His blonde hair and face were spattered with blood. It was like being in a horror film. Ian gulped, put his hand on his shoulder and bent into his face. "What's your name mate?" he shouted. The Mangled Extremity Severity Score (MESS) did not even cross Ian's mind- but perhaps this did not matter for there was not much evidence that it improved outcomes even if it had.

The soldier looked up. Ian did a double take as he saw that he was no older than 18. His eyes were glazed over and he said nothing. As if he had not seen Ian at all, he looked down again. An explosion flashed nearby and Ian dropped to the ground. He felt the shock wave momentarily alter the pressure in his chest. He instinctively grabbed his shotgun. He then turned back to the casualty after steadying himself.

'ABCDEs!' again he shouted at himself, and then finally remembering the battlefield slant on this mnemonic he shouted 'no CABCDEs!'

C- The catastrophic haemorrhage was dealt with by the tourniquet. He quickly looked up and down for any other signs of massive bleeding. It was widely accepted that in trauma scenarios such as wartime a massive catastrophic haemorrhage kills quicker than an obstructed airway hence why 'C' would come before ABCDE. He would know about it due to an extreme volume of blood spurting out from arteries it if there were a catastrophic haemorrhage, which there was not, so he moved on to 'A'. He exposed the boy's chest and neck.

A- He assessed his airway. It was patent, the boy was muttering to him but was making no sense. Ian had to be aware of cervical spine injury- had the boy been thrown by the blast? He pulled out the relevant kit and taped two sandbags on either side of the boy's head as well as a neck collar. The boy allowed him to do it without too much difficulty- not a good thing as most patients hated how uncomfortable it was. Ian needed to get him onto 100% oxygen in case he was de-saturating- he could not find the oxygen saturations probe.

B- He was breathing- fast, but he nevertheless was breathing. He would have listened with a stethoscope for breath sounds, but he would not have heard anything over the noise. He made a quick attempt to see if the chest expansion was symmetrical, he judged it was. He forgot there was even a test for respiratory rate.

C- Circulation. He took his arm and checked for a radial pulse. His heart was racing at 150 beats per minute, regularly regular. But it was a very weak pulse. Thready. Ian checked him over for other injuries or disabilities. Finding none he looked at him more closely. He was sweating heavily, yet when Ian felt his skin it was clammy. His lips were blue. He squeezed his finger to check for capillary refill, it took longer than 2 seconds for the finger to regain colour.

Alarm bells rang in Ian's mind amongst the other noises which filled it. The boy was in shock and what was worse he was deteriorating. Another explosion. Bang! A mortar round was fired from behind him and made a distant whistle as it dropped towards its target.

D- Disability. The boy's Glasgow Coma Scale score was going down as Ian assessed him across the three domains of Motor (6 points), Voice (5 points) and Eyes (4 points). He did not have time to reassess but in terms of AVPU (alert, responsive to voice, responsive to pain, unresponsive.) He was now only responding to pain when Ian pressed on his supraorbital nerve. He looked like he was falling asleep. Ian worked more quickly, talking to him constantly. He fumbled for his radio, his lifeline to Dr Merlin his lecturer at the Secret Medical School which had helped him so many times before, hoping to god that he would hear him over the noise. "Dr Merlin! I have a casualty in shock! What should I do?" Merlin's voice came over the radio instantly to Ian's heart wrenching relief.

"What are his symptoms? Does he have the symptoms of shock?" Merlin asked.

"Yes- pallor, sweating and clammy skin?" Ian replied.

"What about reduced urinary output?"

"No idea?" Ian pressed the radio to his ear hard- he was annoyed at the question- how did he know what his urinary output was! Bang! Another mortar round.

"Tachypnoea, agitation, restlessness- coma? He has these symptoms?!" Merlin spoke calmly, but more seriously than usual. Bang!

"Yes most of them- he's going into coma I think!" Another explosion went off causing a huge cloud of dust. Ian covered the boy's face to keep the dust away.

"Right, are they associated with tachycardia?" Merlin continued.

"Yes. Heart rate 150," Ian shouted.

"Hypotension and peripheral shutdown?"

"Yes! Yes!" Ian now pressed on his sternum for 5 seconds with his thumb and waited to see the blood return. "His central capillary refill is greater than 3 seconds!" Ian shouted down the headset. Zip-Zip-Zip, bullets raced into the wall he was hiding behind. He glanced over at Jim who was trying to get an artificial airway into his casualty after probably a rapid sequence induction anaesthetic.

"Keep calm boy! Don't lose it now. Some conditions such as pulmonary embolism can mimic shock." Ian rolled his eyes on the verge of panic, surely he was not about to get a lecture- he was not having a PE in the middle of a bloody battlefield! Merlin continued. "The features of shock you are seeing are secondary to general and inadequate tissue perfusion. They are also related to tissue hypoxia and anaerobic tissue metabolism. Has he lost a lot of blood?"

"Yes!" More bullets zipped a few metres above Ian's head. A wall behind him toppled over as armour piercing rounds bit into it.

Merlin continued, "There are three types of shock, hypovolaemic, cardiogenic and distributive. Treat him for hypovolaemia- haemorrhagic shock. Shock due to blood loss!" Ian pressed his earpiece harder into his ear straining every nerve in his body to hear more clearly. He breathed fast. He thought of his mother. Why had he said he would do this? The other radio sounded as the pilot hurried them along. It still seemed a miracle the helicopter had not been hit. The boy was even more unresponsive, almost comatose. Bang!

"What stage of shock is he in?" Merlin asked.

"Stage?!" Ian replied, unsure what he meant.

"How much blood has he lost? Remember the percentage blood loss indicates the stage of shock?!"

Ian did not respond, an explosion meant he had not heard all of the transmission and he was too panicked to get Merlin to say it twice.

"Remember it is like the tennis scoring system? Mellows? 0-15% total body blood loss is stage one, 15-30% blood loss is stage two, 30-40% is stage three?!"

"I don't know!" Ian responded shortly.

"No matter," Merlin replied. Ian listened to further instructions and signalled to some nearby soldiers they needed to get the casualty into the Chinook. The Sergeant in charge started barking orders to some of the men defending Ian's position. Merlin was frantically relaying instructions. "You need to resuscitate this man using principles of damage control. You must prevent the classic triad of death associated with trauma from setting in- that of coagulopathy, hypothermia and acidosis! His loss of warm blood leads to him cooling down, as well as losing vital clotting factors and oxygen carrying capacity from the lack of haemoglobin. Remember permissive hypotension! Do not give him too much fluid or you can make things worse!" Ian frantically tried to get things ready to move.

"Right- so what treatment?" Ian shouted.

"Is he unconscious?"

"He is now." Ian said amongst another explosion. Bang! Bang! Bang! The mortar team fired volleys of rounds now into the distance. Perhaps they were retreating?

"Time is precious. Is he maintaining his airway?" Merlin continued.

"He's snoring!" Ian shouted rustling in the medical bag.

"Ok get in a better airway if he will tolerate it. After CABCDEs, Give 100% oxygen by mask." Ian got out an endo-tracheal tube and inserted it as he had been shown by Jim using a twisting technique. The boy did not cough it up so Ian left it in place. "Good. Well done. Place the patient in the lateral position, raise his legs if you can. Don't use the head down position- that can lead to cerebral or pulmonary haemorrhage." Ian did not know what the 'head down' position was so there was no chance of that. The soldiers by now had arrived with a stretcher and after carefully getting the casualty onto it, made a dash for the Chinook. Most of the equipment was in there.

"Done!" Ian shouted down the radio as he ran alongside it. Bullets had stopped hitting the helicopter now, and they did not whiz past quite so frequently. Perhaps they were forcing them back?

"Good. Get IV lines in- two large bore cannulas in the anterior cubital fossae- other side of the elbows. You'll need to take blood tests for electrolytes, blood gases, haematocrit and PH level and most importantly cross match- you'll have to do that when you are back- or check his dog tags- he should already have a blood type."

"Right..." Ian jotted notes on his rubber glove, as was the done thing in the battlefield.

"This boy ultimately needs blood products with specific ratios of platelets, fresh frozen plasma and packed red cells. Giving him tons of fluids is like filling him up with water- with no oxygen or nutrient carrying ability. But, the heart needs fluid to pump, so some fluid challenges can be useful. Aim for a systolic blood pressure of 90 mmhg with the fluids you give. Are you understanding this boy?"

"Yes I'm doing it- I've got Hartmanns?" Ian did not have time to clarify things he did not quite understand. Another explosion. And another. And a third.

"That's fine, just get on with it. Make sure it is warmed! Cold fluids add to hypothermia! Give around a

500ml fluid challenge and see if he responds. Have you got blood available?"

"Yes!"

"Get some O Negative into him if you don't know his blood type- and remember oxygen transport to the tissues becomes ideal at a haematocrit of 30%. But remember- ultimately this boy is leaking blood from somewhere! He needs the tap turning off, not simply filling up with more blood and fluid! Increasing a patient's blood pressure too much by putting in too much fluid can make them bleed more. Vascular teams liken this to a bath full of water with a running tap and a hole in the bottom of it- the amount of water in the bath puts a pressure on the hole- if a clot forms in that hole and stops the leak, you might shift it away by running more water into the bath and applying more pressure to the hole. Ultimately the tap needs turning off!"

"Ok…" Ian got to work, listening as much as he could as he went. Bang! Another explosion.

"Next the acidosis. Correct the acid- base disturbances if he needs! Infuse insulin and remember to correct the calcium if you are infusing large amounts of blood. Get him on antibiotics early to help prevent infections later which can be devastating post trauma, and get him to corrective or damage control surgery as soon as his condition permits. You might also think about giving some tranexamic acid if it is within 3 hours of the injury, this can help with coagulation! Is that all clear?"

"Yes, clear!" Ian hoped he had heard everything, it was difficult with all the noise. Ultimately he needed to get back to the field hospital, most of what Merlin had said would be done there.

The enemy gunfire increased. Bullets smashed against the armour plating of the Chinook and the 50. Cal gun roared out in retaliation. Ian busily got together everything Merlin had said. Then Ian's heart sank, for again he heard a sound no soldier wishes to hear over the PRR radio. "Man down! Man down!" It was Jim's voice. Ian instinctively jumped up and rushed out of the helicopter. He hoped to god it was not too many more. He was not sure how much more of this he could cope with.

The patrol medic who had met them a few moments earlier was spread-eagled on the floor, unconscious. Blood was spraying from his chest and gurgling out of his mouth. Jim shouted something at him but he was too dazed to register it. "Get me the thoracotomy pack, now!" Jim shouted again, a look of terror gripping his face. Ian snapped out of it the second time. The pack was on the helicopter. He sprinted as fast as he could, knowing that every second was crucial. A bullet whizzed overhead. He was going to get some extra morphine as well. Maybe all they could do was make him comfortable.

But before he reached the helicopter, very suddenly everything in Ian's world became slow and hazy. In this haziness he was aware he could not catch his breath and an intense pain gripped his leg. Why was he on the ground? He clutched his leg. It felt strange, warm and wet. His ears were consumed by a high pitched whistling. He fought to wake up submerged in a confusing but vivid dream which would not release him from its grasp. The pain grew stronger. Someone was shaking him, but who this someone was he could not tell. He noticed how hot the ground was. And a wind gently touched his face. What a gentle wind it was! He had not noticed the wind before!

Ian tried to move his head. He tried to move his body. He had to get up- he needed to get Jim the thoracotomy pack. He could not fail the test. He could not fail it! He was so close! But no matter how long for and how hard he tried, he could not move. He briefly heard someone shouting his name. They shouted louder and something was tied tight around his thigh. A belt? But why had they tied a belt around his thigh? Had he done something wrong? He tried to speak but no words would come from his mouth. His breathing slowed. The voice grew faint. The whistling tinnitus in his ears went quiet. The pain eased. He felt comfortable. He felt frightened.

He felt tired. His eyelids felt very, very heavy. And then everything went dark.

Chapter Two: Medics!

Three months earlier, North East England...

"And physiotherapy to mobilise. Next patient." If it were not for the eagle eyed stare of his current arch enemy, Consultant Cardio-Thoracic Surgeon Mr Daniel Bing- Ian Mellows would have fallen asleep long ago. Sat in the multi-disciplinary team meeting he was so bored that he had counted every light, every light switch, every screw on every light switch, and every wire to every light switch in the room. Twice. Ian was in fact so bored that he wondered about jabbing a pencil into one of his deep blue eyes. At least that would get him out of the meeting, even if it did cost him his sight. But maybe that was a price worth paying, because at this rate he thought the boredom might actually kill him. He pushed his fingers through his wavy hair, and sighed.

Not that he did not think these were important meetings, because they were. But for a medical student with no say or even knowledge to say something worthwhile to be in one for more than about one and a half minutes, was a very cruel joke. A lamp went on at the side of the room, and it was only when the registrar repeated his name for the third time that Ian realised he was being asked to interpret an Xray. "Bugger," he said to himself.

"What has happened to this man Mellows?" The registrar asked.

"Hmmmm…" As was the norm, Ian got up to the front of the room and stood next to the lamp trying as hard as possible to make it look as if he was crucially assessing the subtle differences between the tiniest of tiny image markings. In fact his brain was simply shouting at him that he did not have the faintest idea, over and over and over again. All fifteen sets of eyes were on him- nurses, physios, Occupational Therapists, ward managers, doctors- as he stood totally befuddled. It was like they revelled in the awkwardness, even though half of them in the room could not read an xray themselves. He had always been crap at interpreting xrays, but bearing in mind he was a third year medical student, he had probably only ever had three seminars worth of teaching on them, if that.

"Well…" There looks to be some consolidation on the right-"

"Stop!" From the back of the room, Daniel Bing stared at Ian with such distain you would have thought he had just stolen a dying child's milk. "Let me guess, you are crap at interpreting xrays- as is every other medical student. Tell him how to do it would you bitch." By bitch he was referring to the registrar. Ian would have blushed, but he was so used to Mr Daniel Bing being a scrawny, bullying idiot- that he simply stood and stared back at him, seething. The registrar was also used to this and Ian wondered if he actually embraced it slightly. The registrar turned to Ian, and began to teach.

"Start by identifying that the xray is the correct patient's. As in, this is Mr Tony Scott, aged 65. Next comment on the type of xray. Is it taken from Posterior Anterior? Or is it Anterior Posterior? Remember in Anterior Posterior films, or AP films- you cannot really comment on the heart, for it appears enlarged- simply look for the letters AP or PA usually in a top corner." Ian vaguely remembered this fact, but was glad the registrar had reminded him of it.

"Comment next on the penetration. Is the Xray penetrated ok? You should just be able to see spinous processes through the myocardium and so on."

"Right," Ian retorted.

"Hurry up please, we don't have all day!" Mr Bing ejected from the back of the room. Both registrar and Ian ignored him amongst the deadly silence of the room. A ward sister coughed.

"After checking the penetration, follow ABCDE of xrays. A=Airway area. Comment on the oesophagus and trachea- are they central or deviated? B= Breathing. Look at the lung markings. Count the number of ribs- as in the anterior ribs which are to the side- not the more obvious ones centrally. There should be 6-8 ribs shown in between the clavical and the central head of the diaphragm. If there are more, the patient is hyperexpanded as in a pneuomothorax or emphysema. C- Circulation. If it is a PA film, comment on the myocardium- is it enlarged? Comment on if you can see the knuckle of the aorta. D- Diaphragm. This should be higher on the right than the left, and there is usually a gas bubble underneath it. E- Everything else. Comment on the bones, the soft tissues, breast shadows and so on. Have a stab at if it is a normal or abnormal xray.

"If you are unsure what the condition is- do not guess- simply comment in radiological terms- say there is a diffuse white shadow over the left lower zone for example." He handed a sheet to Ian. "There's a summary sheet, read up on it." Ian folded it and shoved it clumsily into his pocket.

"You should know what the xray diagnosis is at your stage Mellows!" Mr Bing shouted rudely.

"Oh for god's sake," Ian murmured to himself angrily, fed up with the usual onslaught of questions.

"What was that?" Mr Bing stood up and leant over the desk threateningly. Everyone in the room looked at the floor, or the ceiling or anywhere else but in Mr Bing's direction. Except one female junior doctor who looked at him like a Cheshire cat. Ian was sure she had been shagging Bing at one point, sad desperate girl. Ian had not meant to say it quite so loudly. Mr Bing's eyes nearly popped out of their sockets they were so wide. "What was that boy!" he exclaimed, even louder than the first time.

"Nothing," Ian said as argumentatively as he possibly could. Oh how he hated this man!

"Outside!" Bing screamed.

"Sorry?" Ian retorted.

"Get outside! Now!" Bing gesticulated aggressively with his finger towards the door. Ian, accepting of his fate, walked as calmly as he could, passing the accusatory eyes who now looked at him as if he had taken the child's milk and pissed in it in front of them. Bing took him to the end of the ward. His face was bright red and his temples pulsating. Ian thought he might give himself a stroke.

He glanced down the wide white ward corridor at the nurses' station which was bustling with eavesdropping fellow students all pretending not to listen to his telling off. A nurse shook her head. In the side room he heard a man calling out for help. The stench of urine mixed with disinfectant filled his nostrils.

Maybe it was last week's comment about Mr Bing's abrupt bedside manner which had done it. Maybe it was when he said he did not find Mr Bing's jokes funny. Maybe it was the constant look of hatred he displayed on his face whenever this poor excuse for a human being taught him which had finally made Mr Bing flip. Ian did not know. What he did know was that this Cardio-Thoracic Surgeon was angry, and it made him frightened.

"Mellows, you are a filthy, downright despicable excuse for a medical student." Spit flew out of his mouth and hit Ian in the face. He wiped it away fighting hard to appear unbothered. He looked up and down the broad, slightly receding man as sweat dripped off his round face and made drips on his shirt. Grey hairs dotted about his bushy brown eyebrows, and his pointy nose stuck out like a sparrow's beak. Ian had never hated anyone quite so much as this before. He made him feel sick. The poor souls who had to work with him all year! At least his placement was only a few months, and it was almost over!

"I am going to write a personal letter to the head of your medical school suggesting that you are thrown out!" His eyes formed into narrow slits and his nostrils flared with contempt. He thrust an accusatory finger at Ian's nose. "Never in my time as a surgeon have I come across such an imbecile! You will amount to nothing. Nothing!"

"Thank you kindly, Mr Bing. I think so little of your opinion that to be called an imbecile by you probably means I'm actually doing just fine." Ian did not know how to respond to such injustice so turned to sarcasm. To say the least, this made Mr Bing's head explode and he was subsequently thrown off the ward with the threat of death if he ever so much as looked at the angry surgeon again. He probably should report him for that. But why bother? Things would not change.

Ian marched out of D Wing fuming, shaking with rage. He headed straight for his personal tutor's office. Knowing what he did of Mr Bing, he would write that letter. Unfortunately the medical profession seemed riddled with people like him who bullied their way through life. This was not the first time an event like this had happened, and it was not just him whom it had happened to. In Ian's experience it seemed all medical students should expect to be patronised, bullied and ridiculed, just for being medical students.

Ian was fed up. He hoped that Mr Vesely was in his office. It was coming up to lunch, hopefully he could catch him before afternoon surgery. He drew up to the secretary's office door and knocked impatiently.

"Come in!" A high pitched voice ejected from behind the frosted glass. Ian pushed the cool metal handle which squeaked against the NHS hardboard.

"Ian my dear!" the lady smiled warmly. "How can I be of assistance?" Jean, a middle aged and well-spoken lady sat behind her desk as normal. She rested down the Dictaphone she had been typing letters from.

"Is Mr Vesely available? I need to speak to him." Ian's adrenaline pulsed and he could feel a large sweat patch on his back. He tried to take some deep breaths.

"You're in luck. He is here, I'll check if he can see you." She picked up the white telephone receiver on her desk and pushed a button which made a bleeping sound. "Mr Vesely, Ian Mellows here to see you- would you be alright for him to... Yes of course I'll tell him." She replaced the receiver with a click. "He is just speaking with a colleague, wait outside his door." She smiled, picked up the black Dictaphone again and continued typing up a pile of letters.

Ian walked out of her office and turned a few yards down the corridor to the three orange chairs which stood outside the polished door which was the entrance to Mr Vesely's office. Ian could hear his soft voice behind the wood. Sitting down to wait he wondered how he could put his latest run in to his tutor.

Mr Vesely was a surgeon Ian had never quite worked out. He knew him well, yet also felt there were large amounts about him which he was hidden from. Despite this, he was the one authoritative medical person he felt he could trust, and more importantly, who would stand up for him. He was also one of the only humble surgeons and doctors he knew and had had many conversations with him about the failings of medical school and his frustrations with the system. Mr Vesely would sit contentedly behind his desk and listen to Ian's many rants, offering snippets of advice without ever agreeing or disagreeing with him.

The tall, wiry man of about fifty always bore a grin throughout his interactions with Ian. Ian never knew why this was but always supposed it was merely his facial expression. This plastic surgeon was someone whom he had great respect for, as many others in the hospital and medical school did.

So when Ian was finally called into his office, what Mr Vesely said to him was not something he had expected. Blinded by the bright sunlight reflected off the puddles of rain spattered on the roofs directly out of the window behind Mr Vesely's armchair, Ian stood quite confused. "I have just been on the phone with Mr Bing and I am in absolute agreement with him."

"Sorry?" It was like someone had punched him hard in the stomach.

"I am in agreement with Mr Bing, you are different from the other students." Mr Vesely smiled, pushing his hand through his blonde hair. Ian felt the blood rush into his face and his heart beat hard against his chest.

"But sir- this is my third year- I was coming here for help in not being thrown out!" He must be joking. He was having a sarcastic turn. But stern in the face, Mr Vesely's deep green eyes pierced him in a way which he knew was neither sarcastic nor humorous. Was the whole world against him?

"Ah but you see, Mellows, what Bing sees as a problem, I see as an advantage. And for that reason, I would like you to follow me." With that, Mr Vesley stood up out of his chair and walked over to the wall. He pressed a light switch next to the heavy looking book case.

All of a sudden, the book case made a deep whirring sound, and moved electronically away from the wall, revealing another room behind it. It was like something from a 'Star Trek' film. A *secret* room? In a hospital? Ian had never heard of such a thing. "Follow me." Vesely said. He walked through the opening and led into a hallway, which led to another door- this time made of steel. He knocked on it with a clanging sound, and someone shouted 'enter' from the other side. It really was most bizarre. What was this place? Vesely opened the door and led into another office, just like his own. It was large, full of books and old paintings. Ian followed on nervously.

Occupying the office was a very old man who must have been nearly ninety. Wisps of grey hair dotted about his beard and he was wearing a dark, but very smart suit. He looked very good for an elderly man- perhaps Ian had misjudged his age- maybe he was a smoker and looked older than he actually was. He sat at a large old desk and had a large picture of the queen on the wall above the fireplace behind his desk, and a huge map of the world like ones used by ships in the Royal Navy to the right. He also had various historical items on a shelf by the window, including what looked like an old Hitler Youth knife, as well as a revolver from the First World War.

"Ian mellows this is Dr Klaus Merlin. Please take a seat." Mr Vesely ushered.

"How do you do," the man said. Ian shook his hand firmly. His eyes smiled warmly.

"The reason we have called you in here is to offer you the shot at a job we have lined up next year." Me Vesely said.

"Oh right?" Ian said bemused. He was being offered a job? Not being thrown out? He smiled excitedly. He knew Vesely was a decent bloke!

"This is not any sort of job, might I add, it will require your full and undivided attention, and some slightly different training to what you are used to." Mr Vesely continued.

"Ok..." Ian wondered where this was going, he was hoping to apply to a London hospital and get out of the north, but would have been happier to get any job out of medicine the way his degree was going. "What is it, if you don't mind me asking?" Ian was sat upright with his hands in his lap, trying to look polite.

"Please sign this, before I can say anything to you." Dr Merlin said firmly.

This seemed a curious thing to ask, Ian thought. Dr Merlin handed over a form, which had the crest of her majesty's government on it, the title of which read, 'official secrets act'. "Your developed vetting will take further time after this, but for now this form of secrecy is acceptable to us."

Developed Vetting? That was something spies had? Ian signed the form, for what was the problem in signing an official secrets act, Merlin and Vesely certainly had his curiosity? He was used to confidentiality in medicine, and was a very proud Brit. Grand supporter of queen and country. Or something like that anyway.

Dr Merlin finally started to whisper, "Thank you. We are offering you a job as a doctor in the British Secret Service."

"The Secret Service!" Ian ejected excitedly. He realised this had come across perhaps too excited, so immediately attempted to appear more relaxed.

"Yes. The Secret Service." The two men sat quite still, looking at him seriously. "We have requirements for doctors just as any other branch of the military or police does. We feel you may be suitable to work for us. You must pass an assessment to start off with, conducted by me- and then you will be taken out of medical school training at times of our choosing in order to complete specific training requirements. You must be aware that part of your training will be in a hazardous environment abroad such as the Middle East or Africa." Ian's eyes widened, and his pupils dilated gleefully. Vesely! He knew Vesely was different! What a fantastic opportunity!

He needed very little persuading. This is exactly the sort of thing he wanted to do, this was the excitement he was after. This was being a proper doctor, not an administrative clerk like so many juniors seemed to be.

"And if I pass the training?" Ian asked.

"You will start full time with us at the end of the year. Presuming that year is passed successfully."

"Where do I sign?" Ian asked, and Merlin handed another document to him, with 'Secret' in red letters written across the front of it. He did not need to ask any more questions. This was it.

Chapter Three: Tests

3 months until Iraq

After signing the document, Merlin and Vesely gave Ian an envelope with a time and place to report for his 'assessment'. He then had to burn the letter. He found a private place, and opened it carefully.

Tommorrow morning, 0830, Tynemouth Priory. Revise basic physiology for the test.

After a sleepless night of cramming old physiology text books, Ian turned up at exactly that place. He had been here before, it was some sort of old priory that monks used hundreds of years ago but also had some sort of cold war radar station in it, strategically looking out over the North Sea. It was a cold day, and in the distance there were some dark clouds. A large oil tanker chugged out of the river Tyne into the wide grey ocean, waves lapping rhythmically against its sides. Presently, colourful clouds hung in spirally wisps over the tall, old ruin while red fiery beams of sunlight dotted down onto the gravestones of the cemetery. Ian thought it would certainly rain soon though. "Ian Mellows?" Another old man who looked like a janitor met him. "Yes? Hi." Ian smiled at the attendant who said hello back with a face as lively as a particularly monotonous plank of wood. Were you supposed to say 'hi' to these people? It was a test after all? He gestured for Ian to follow him. Thinking him slightly odd, Ian eagerly followed on into the grassed cemetery and up to a heavy wooden door. He stepped inside. His footsteps echoed on the stone floor and candles lined the walls as they made their way downstairs. Dr Merlin was standing in a cold stone room waiting for him. In it, was a long desk, a lectern as well as a power point projector. It was most out of place in such an old building. Merlin took Ian a little off guard. "Thank you Alf." Merlin said to the man, who promptly left without a word, hovering slightly in front of the doorway. "Right. This is your one and only test, and knowledge is not the only part of it that counts- balls mellows- this jobs takes balls- and that's what I want you to show me. Follow me."

At least Merlin would not stand on ceremony. Merlin led him down a passageway at the end of the room to the right. They descended several hundred steps, down and down and down into the depths of the cliffs. Ian thought they might be under the sea by now, and his legs started to ache.

All of a sudden, Merlin stopped. He pulled a rusty old lever sticking out of the wall. Ian could only just make it out in the dim light. It made a clunking sound, and some lights came on above them. Ian squinted, adjusting to the new brightness. "Had much on this week?" Ian nervously asked trying to start some sort of conversation. Dr Merlin did not reply, walking on in through a rusty old door which had swung open. He beckoned Ian to follow.

The room they had entered was another stone chamber with a few small barred windows in one of the walls. They were near the beaches at the bottom of the cliff. In front of them was a metal table, its head against the wall. Dr Merlin looked at him and walked over to a separate side table which was covered with a white sheet. He removed the sheet and revealed another metal table with several tools on it. Scalpels, hammers, saws- Ian was baffled as to what he was about to do. "Today phase one of the test is called, 'what should have been done?' "

"Right..." Ian retorted feeling jittery. Merlin walked to the end of the table against the wall and pushed a green button. A door in the wall, concealed from view, began to open. Ian's blood ran cold. It opened further and further, and as it did so a slab slowly moved out of the wall onto the table. On this slab was what Ian instantly knew to be a dead body, covered with a sheet.

"People who ask to be buried in the beautiful Tynemouth Priory cemetery do so in the knowledge they will be subject to their post mortem here in which a medical student will be involved. They accept this as the desire to be buried in such a beautiful spot makes this merely a formality," his eyes pierced Ian's. "Today you will perform a post mortem on this patient, finding out what killed them, as well as investigating their body tissues. I will test you as you go." He smirked. "You get started and I'll come and help in a few moments, I'll be in contact in the meantime via a video link. Everything you need is on that table. Clear?"

Ian stood dumbstruck.

"Good," Dr Merlin affirmed. Before Ian could protest he had marched out of the room and slammed the door.

Ian stood still, feeling a little sick. The door slamming sounded a metal clang up and down the passageway outside the room. A seagull fluttered its wings at the window, temporarily blotting out the beams of sunlight which entered the small chamber. Ian could not bear to uncover the sheet over the body. The waves washing against the beach crashed in the distance.

Elephant, still unrevealed in the room, all Ian could feel was guilt. It was not right he was to start the post mortem! He had had no training! Apart from dissection in previous years, he had little idea where to start. It felt somewhat disrespectful. But Dr Merlin had said- they were consented to this. And anyhow, he had signed up to it. This is what he was being tested on- they had said it would not be easy. There was no backing out now. If he could not do this, what else could he not do?

"Get on with it, haven't got all day boy." Dr Merlin's voice interrupted his pangs of conscience and the eerie stillness. It came from a speaker somewhere. Ian searched up and down the room but could not find for toffee where it was. He had that horrible feeling you get when you know you are being watched.

"Okay!" he said aloud. Where was Dr Merlin watching from? Ian walked over to the metal table and inspected the objects on it nervously. Mostly there were cutting implements- scalpels and the like- but what caught his eye was a red and blue book. *'How to perform a post mortem: The idiot's guide.'*

Ian had dissected cadavers in his first two years so essentially this was familiar, but performing someone's post mortem? The idiot's guide!

He rubbed his finger over the half fallen apart book and opened it. It was well used and a cloud of dust flew out from between the pages. *'Chapter one: The brain,'* Ian read on. It described in just enough detail for him to understand what to do, but not enough to put him off or intimidate him. *'Place the head on a block, or ideally egg cup shaped stand, and make an incision behind the ears, ear to ear. Be careful to make this discreet- relatives will not thank you if you leave their relative looking mangled- they may wish to see the body after your actions and before a religious ritual. Be delicate.'* 'Better get on with it'- Ian thought. He picked up the knife and walked over to the sheet. He lifted it and folded it down just so it rested on the chest.

A man lay before him, mouth open in an O shape and his face a dull grey colour. He did not look old. Ian took a deep breath and attempted the cut. The knife was blunt. He simply scraped a few grey hairs off. On closer inspection, it revealed that he had in fact tried to use the chisel which was for prizing open bone. He blushed sickeningly. He tried again with a proper scalpel, this time successfully. It slid through the skin and hair ear to ear. Having got through, (rather neatly even if he said so himself,) the initial layer of scalp to bone he picked up the drill. He turned it on and put it to the revealed bone. It squealed like a dentist's as shards of bone flicked this way and that. One hit him on the cheek, and he brushed it away quickly. He put on some eye protection, and continued. He placed the chisel between the crack, and hammered open the skull. A small pool of blood fell onto the floor. He screwed up his face but tried to ignore his repulsion scientifically. He carefully took away the piece of skull he had removed. Cutting the medulla and dura matter, and the protective layer of the brain attached to the skull, Ian removed it and held it in his hand. How bizarre to be holding someone's brain!

'Slice brain like you would cheese and weigh it. Inspect specimens from each lobe under the microscope for abnormalities.' The idiot's guide! Ian took the brain over to the side of the room and took up a knife. He found it easier to think of as a piece of meat, although after a while imagined eating the piece of meat and wretched. The stench grew stronger.

Ian noticed a slice of brain appearing darker than the others. He decided to put it aside to examine under a microscope later. Next he made an incision over the chest in a T-shape. He looked at the saw, and picked it up. This bit made him feel sick. With some difficulty, and much spraying bone- Ian sawed open the ribs in a square segment, just like the book said. He lifted the front of rib cage off attached to the sternum, to replace at the end of the procedure. The abdomen was full of blood and other fluid. Ian screwed up his nose at the smell, but continued to dissect according to the book. *'Take out both heart and lungs, hold up and inspect by the tongue.'* He had seen a post mortem once during medical school, and remembered this. He cut away at the ligaments and vessels attaching everything together, and pulled out the heart and lungs with a slurping sound, holding them up by the tongue. He tried not to drip blood on his feet. Ian thought this somewhat disrespectful, but Merlin clearly thought nothing of it watching from wherever he was. "Well done boy. Good," his voice came over the speaker again.

Ian continued feeling encouraged. He placed them on the metal table and took a scalpel to the heart to slice it. "Tell me how the heart works Mr Mellows." Merlin then asked.

"How it works?"

"Yes. How it works. Physiologically. My memory needs refreshing." Ian knew that was total rubbish, but reached into the depths of his first year to try to remember, ignoring the patronising way in which he had been asked.

"Well, the heart has four chambers. The left and right atria, which are thin walled, and the two more thick walled and muscular left and right ventricles."

"Good. And what are the ventricles and atria separated by?" This time, what Merlin had said was not over the microphone, but in person- for he had walked into the room- maybe Ian had taken longer than he had thought? Merlin held up the heart and showed Ian a band of connective tissue.

"That is the annulous fibrosis. It prevents electrical conduction between the atria and ventricles, except through the atrio-ventricular node or AV node."

Ian stood quietly as Merlin picked up the scalpel. He continued to dissect- content he had satisfied him so far.

"Continue," Merlin added, looking down the end of his glasses. Ian sighed, thinking back again.

"Well, the inner surface of the heart is lined by a thin layer of cells called the endocardium, which is thrombogenic and stops blood clotting."

"And what is this?" Merlin pointed to a thin fibrous sac which covered the whole of the bloody heart.

"That is the pericardium." Gosh he was surprised to remember this, normally he forgot most things he read only once.

"And what does it do?" Merlin continued.

"Well, it contains lubricating fluid and helps protect the heart from damage caused by friction- oh and prevents excessive enlargement."

"Good. Good. Tell me about the heart valves."

"Well, blood flows from the right atrium into the right ventricle via the tricuspid AV valve and from the left atrium to the left ventricle via the mitral AV valve. The valves open and shut as a result of pressure differences on either side of them. If an AV valve gets stenosed it is narrowed and makes ventricular filling inefficient. Stenotic valves increase the afterload and therefore make the ventricles work harder. Incompetent valves do not close properly and leak or in medical terms regurgitate," surely this would be enough for Merlin?

"Good. Lastly tell me about the electrical currents in the heart." This was particularly woolly in Ian's mind, but he would have a stab nonetheless. He had glanced over this page quickly.

"Well, the impulse is started in the sinoatrial node... and it moves down to the atrio-ventricular node- and bundle of His."

"Well, that's an undetailed explanation. The wave of contraction starts in the sinoatrial node and is modulated by autonomic nerves. The impulse activates atrial myocytes via the gap junctions within the intercalated discs? Ring any bells?"

"Err- yes, a bit."

"The contraction goes through the atrial muscle to the AV node, where it is delayed very momentarily to allow atrial contraction to complete ventricular filling. Rapid activation is then required through the ventricles in order to pump the blood effectively, so fast conducting myocytes in the bundle of His, as you correctly identified, and the purkinje fibres, evenly distribute the conduction impulse across the inner surface of both ventricles. This electrical current is what we can detect on an ECG, as I am sure you are aware." Ian was very aware. He was beginning to wonder if in fact this medical education was going to be any different to normal, despite him starting the post mortem?

"Good. We are running out of time still for I wish to get onto teaching you with a live patient. But first tell me briefly how the lungs work."

Ian wondered what he would have to do with a live patient! "Air goes in through the trachea and divides down the two main bronchi. These further divide into bronchioles which lead to respiratory bronchioles which then lead on to the alveolar ducts and sacs, the walls of which form alveoli and contain only epithelial cells. Airways from the trachea to the respiratory bronchioles are lined with cilia or tiny hairs. They also contain goblet cells and submucosal glands which secrete mucus. These tiny hairs or cilia, beat the mucus up towards the mouth. Anything which interferes with either the cilia or the mucus function such as in cystic fibrosis, asthma or smoking lead to recurrent infections. Mucus contains substances that protect the airways from pathogens, such as antitrypsins, lysozyme, and immunoglobulin A." Ian was quite impressed with himself. His cramming had done the job!

"Good. Very good. And tell me about surfactant?"

"Secreted by type 2 pneumocytes, it helps prevent the alveoli from collapsing. It is produced by the fetus between 24 to 28 weeks, and therefore can be the reason prematurely born babies struggle to breath if they are born earlier."

"Good. And bearing in mind oxygen and other gases diffuse between the lungs and the blood stream via the alveolar capillary membrane, how is breathing controlled?"

"Well, mostly via the respiratory centre in the brain, composed of differing sets of neurones in the pons and medulla. These control normal breathing, but are regulated by chemoreceptors and lung receptors and descending input from the pneumotaxic centre in the pons. Breathing is generally responsive to the partial pressure of carbon dioxide dissolved in blood. An increase in PACO2 causes ventilation to rise in an almost linear fashion."

"Ok. Good." Merlin looked at him pensively. "Very good indeed." Why did he keep complimenting him?

"Next the kidneys- tell me about them quickly."

"Well, the kidneys help to maintain the composition of extracellular body fluids and regulate electrolytes such as sodium, potassium, calcium and magnesium- as well as maintaining the correct acid-base balance and correct body water content. Blood is filtered by capillaries in the kidneys, situated in the glomerulus and the composition of what is filtered out of these capillaries is modified in the nephrons. The average urine output is 1.5litres per day, although this can fall to under 1 litre a day and increase to almost 20 litres a day."

"Which I am sure you agree, is a lot of piss!" Merlin laughed, holding up one of the kidneys.

"Right. Done. I know what was wrong with them. Phase one complete. Phase two. Follow me." And before Ian could have asked what had caused the death, or anything else, Merlin had disappeared out of the cold stone room, along a passageway into the depths of this secret medical school. What was phase two to be?

Chapter Four: Phase 2 Tests

Dr Merlin led Ian out of the post mortem room, back up the stone stairway, out the heavy door and into the priory forecourt, apparently the ruin of a church. Merlin had climbed the stairs quickly and Ian was out of breath when they reached the top. This man must have been younger than ninety! The sky had become very grey and the wind had picked up to a howl. Drops of rain pitter-pattered about them and gradually these grew larger, beating down hard against his jacket. He was soaked through within a couple of minutes as they walked across the lush green grass towards the cliffs edges. It was freezing. Merlin had put a brolly up and appeared totally unphased by the downpour, standing there in his tweed suit. Ian felt wimpy standing next to him moaning about being wet. He wrapped his jacket tighter around his neck as dampness soaked through to his feet. What were they waiting for?

"Right, hope you don't have a fear of flying, Ian?" Before Ian had a chance to answer, Merlin continued. "Good! There's an offshore oil rig about 45 minutes helicopter journey away- there's a patient we need to sort out. The area is secure, this is a civilian mission."

Ian stood still. He had never been in a helicopter! How exciting, but what would he be expected to do? What a way to learn medicine! Merlin walked further out into the blustery wind and driving rain to gaze out over the sea. Ian had not heard it due to the wind, but through the clouds and mist, lo and behold a helicopter appeared. This was real! A deep rumble met his ears as it grew closer. It was a yellow helicopter bearing 'coast guard' written in black along its side. It slowly came to land with its green and red flashing lights blearing underneath it. Merlin waved a hello to the pilot, who nodded back and slid open the side door ushering them both in. Ian reached up to the handle and pulled himself up. He was enchanted. Merlin shut the door and handed him a head set. "Ready to go David!" Merlin said to the pilot. "Roger Roger, Klaus." The pilot responded. Before Ian knew what was happening, the helicopter had taken off. The cliffs ebbed away into the distance far below. Endless rough seas engulfed them.

Although he had not had a chance to answer Merlin's earlier question, he was no fan of heights and tried not to look out of the window for fear of being sick. The helicopter lurched this way and that against the wind. "Are we ok flying in this weather?" Ian turned to Merlin and asked, trying to hide his trembling, sweaty hands. Merlin turned to him and smiled. "Why yes of course! Can't let a little bad weather get in the way my lad.

Remember you'll have to parachute out of one of these at some point if you pass this assessment!"

This did not fill Ian with confidence. Battling against the wind and driving rain, on the helicopter flew over the ice cold North Sea. Ian forced himself to remain calm. He could not show fear if this old man Merlin did not! What sort of a first impression was it if he broke down over a helicopter ride. As the flight went on he thought he might begin to relax, but all he could do was feel sick.

Before he knew it they reached it, a massive metal structure standing tall in the middle of the ocean. Ian could see it through the battering rain on the helicopter windows. He wondered how man had contemplated building such a thing, so far out to sea. He leant over further to get a better view out of the window. The pilot got on the radio, "The gusts are pretty terrible- this could be a rough landing!"

"No problems David, all the more exciting eh, Ian?" He leaned over and slapped Ian on the back. Ian thought he might vomit, wondering how green he looked. But he could not vomit, it would be too embarrassing and he would probably fail. He felt a lurch in his stomach. The helicopter gradually dipped lower and lower. Suddenly they dropped several metres. Ian grabbed onto the nearest bit of metal and held on tight to his safety belt. The rig became visible in the front window of the helicopter now, large and imposing. They began to rise again. "It's too rough to land, we'll have to do a wire descent."

"Wire descent?" Ian gasped. Merlin did not bat an eyelid, but threw a harness at Ian, leaning across to open the slide door. "Woah! What are you doing!" Ian interjected as fear shot through his body making him tense all his muscles against the side of the helicopter.

"This is part of your test. Either prepare to be lowered or if you do not want to, sit back and we will drop you back on the coast, failed. Is that what you wish?" He looked blankly at Ian, putting on a harness himself. Was Merlin seriously going to be lowered out of this helicopter? At his age? In a tweed suit?

Get a grip, Ian said to himself. "No! No." Ian retorted, trying to summon the courage to find the right way round to his harness. Merlin opened the side door. He gave him the medical bag. Wind and rain burst in howling loudly against the helicopter. Ian fought wildly now to put the harness on and attach himself to something.

"You go first, I'll follow. Your head set will transmit still so leave it on in case we need to talk to you." Ian's adrenaline pumped around his veins so fast he thought he might fly out of the door. Merlin reached across and pulled a steel wire from a crank outside the door and attached it to Ian's harness. He gave it a tug. "Good to go David!"

"Righto!" The pilot retorted.

"Now just sit on the edge of the helicopter, and swing yourself out over the edge."

"Do what?" Ian muttered, panting heavily.

"You heard me. I thought you would be less wimpy Ian, now do as I say you are holding us up, the patient below is very ill." He pushed Ian towards the edge.

"No wait, I'll do it." Ian braced himself against the door, he was not going to move for anything. But before he knew what was happening he felt a heavy shove at his back, and he was spinning on a wire, dangling above the roaring sea, stomach in his throat. Rain and wind howled against his face and he could hardly hear the helicopter the weather was so intense. He stared terrified at the nothingness below and tensed every muscle in his body. The waves must have been 15 foot high, crashing against the sturdy steel structure of the oil rig far below. He was level with the control tower of the rig, and people waved at him from inside. He did not wave back, for both his hands were gripping so tightly to the steel wire that lowered him he thought they might bleed. Slowly but surely, he was lowered down. He swung about in the wind like a conquer on a string towards a platform with a huge letter 'H' landing pad on it. He shut his eyes tight. This was not happening! Eventually, he felt his legs touch down on firm concrete, and a man came and unclipped him. Relief flushed through him.

The man wore a hard hat and grubby boiler suit, and bore a smile. The wire was pulled back up, and Ian waited for Merlin to descend. He could hardly hear the helicopter now. After some minutes, Merlin did not descend. He heard something over the radio set, and his blood ran cold. He should have torn up the wretched letter Vesely gave him. Damned Vesely! "It will take another ten minutes for me to get down its so unsteady up here- you go and deal with the casualty, I'll talk you through it over the radio set and come in when I can. Ok?"

Ian wondered about not responding, perhaps he would think the radio set was broken and would have to come down himself. He did say if the radio was working ok?

"Good," Merlin uttered and before he knew it Ian was ushered off into the depths of the oil rig. He felt terribly nervous, he had never treated a patient alone before. Not to mention all the floors below him were made of metal meshes. One could see the crashing sea far below- it was almost like there was no floor at all if one unfocused their eyes. Damn his fear of heights! Ian tried not to look down and stared at the man's back in front. They went down some sets of steps, and then entered into the mainframe of the rig.

Ian was confronted by a middle aged, bald man sitting on a chair in the middle of an office- who appeared to be the patient. He was surrounded by a couple of other rig workers trying to calm him down. Papers and pens and bits of equipment were strewn all over the place and the men all looked tired as if the sea had been battering them all directly. The patient on the chair looked terribly ill. Ian could not pinpoint why, he just did. He was reported to have a fever. He was clearly agitated and confused, pushing away the men around him, his eyes not really focusing. Merlin asked Ian to take his pulse. Ian approached the man carefully and tried to introduce himself. The man fixated on him wide eyed, and shoved him away. "He's been doing this for forty minutes!" A workman said. Another man went forward to try to get him to calm down, asking if he'd let the doctor see him.

"No! No! Get away! Get away!" The man shouted, eyes bursting and veins pulsating.

"You got anything you can give him, doc? An injection or something to calm him down?" The rig medic asked.

Ian wondered. Someone had said to him before to be cautious about sedating agitated patients he was sure of it, but he could not quite remember what they had said. The patient picked up the chair and started swinging it around the room at the other workers, a look of fury in his eyes. "Do something doc!" One of the other men said. The headset buzzed and Ian heard Merlin's voice.

"What's happening lad?"

"He's very aggressive- sweating and nervous! Should I give him something to restrain him?"

"What do you think?" Dr Merlin asked inquisitively. Ian did not want to be asked what he thought, he wanted to be told what to do!

"I don't know! He maybe could do with a sedative of some sort, just to calm him down? But I can't give that?" Surely he was not expected to treat the man? A medical student!

"Well I'll leave it up to you Ian. This is a test after all. You have vials of Haloperidol or Midazolam to give to him if you like? Will make him easier to tackle and cannulate and so on if you like?"

Ian could not work out if this was a trick question. Was he really supposed to treat him? "But I am not sure what the cause is, if he has a head injury then the sedation might mask if he deteriorates?" He wished he could remember what that person had warned him of in sedating patients.

"Has he got a head injury?" Ian asked the workmen. 'Not sure,' was the response, they had only just come across him. He took medications for thyroid was all they knew. "I'll leave it to you Mellows. Your decision."

Ian wondered whether it really was up to him. He had never even seen a sedative administered, let alone given one himself. Suddenly two of the men launched themselves forward and grabbed the man, wrestling him to the floor. Flurries of shouts and screams amongst an unravelling brawl ensued. "Do it now doc, while he's on the floor! Stab him with a needle to calm him down! Do it doc!" The rig medic shouted at Ian.

Ian was sweating profusely, and his heart beat hard. He really was not sure what the right answer was. Maybe the men had dealt with this before? They probably knew it to be right? He went over to the man who was now pinned down by three men and said, "Calm down mate, I'm here to help you ok." He said to the men he would just check his pulse first, and then would give an injection- he'd have to look it up first though for the right dose. The rig medic rolled his eyes and shouted, "Just get on with it, doc! You new or something?" Ian ignored him. Whilst he was on the floor, with the men still telling him to hurry up and give the injection, he did a swift examination.

The man's heart was racing and the beat was irregularly irregular- tachycardia and Atrial Fibrillation. "What's he been like before this, does anyone know?" Ian asked.

"He's had D and V for a few days previous to this," the medic reported. "Look stop faffing doc, just give him the injection!" Ian noticed the patient had a clear swelling in his neck- perhaps a goitre? Ian thought hard. Some sort of infection? He tried to elicit some more signs, and asked further about the history. The workers looked at him bemused for asking, but knew he took regular medication for his thyroid, but was not sure if he had any history of diabetes, epilepsy, asthma, strokes or heart disease. Ian's brain whirred as he attempted to formulate a plan. Sweat formed on his brow. The man was calming down slightly, so maybe he did not need to sedate him? "Doc give him the injection now before he hurts himself or one of us!" the medic shouted again, and the other men nodded their heads and made sounds of agreement. Ian gave in, went to the medical bag, and searched for the Haloperidol.

But before he could do anything, saved by the bell, Merlin walked in, drenched.

"Did you sedate him?" Merlin asked, taking off his jacket.

"No, not yet- just working out if he needs it or not?" Ian lied. If he had not turned up, he would probably have given him the injection. At least having Merlin there was a medical mind who would know either way what to do. As soon as he entered, all the other men seemed to calm down, and the atmosphere relaxed. Experienced help was here!

"Good! Do what you can with any patient who is confused before turning to drugs, despite what other people will tell you. If you sedate a patient, you cannot tell if their consciousness is deteriorating from the drug you have given, or from a pathology- perhaps an expanding brain haemorrhage which will kill them if nothing is done about it. The classic patient to be careful with, who is very difficult to know the right decision in, is a drunk patient with a head injury. Is it alcohol causing their aggression and confusion- or is it the head injury? Don't get me wrong Ian, sometimes sedation is all you can do to calm a patient down- but often being unthreatening and allowing the patient to calm down and become used to you and not scared is more helpful. Tackling a confused and aggressive man with aggression usually only makes the situation worse. Use sedation as a last resort." Ian nodded, thank god Merlin had turned up! Those workers would have probably made him give it! He felt wronged by their panics. The workers took no notice they had nearly forced him to wrongly sedate the man, but had calmed down a lot since Merlin's entrance. They obviously knew him and that he would sort things out. Ian himself had relaxed, but nevertheless was keen to find out what was wrong with the patient.

"Anyhow, Ian, what is wrong with this man?" Merlin asked.

"Well I'm not sure? He has signs of heart problems and a neck swelling, but I can't see what would cause this outburst?"

"Think boy. Irregularly irregular pulse?"

" Myocardial infarction or a stroke due to thrombus? Though there is no signs of heart or vascular disease evident on examination," Ian said as if he was in an OSCE.

"Not a bad suggestion. But incorrect. Think about the swelling in the neck." Merlin handed him a box. "Look at his regular medication. Ian read the front, *'Levothyroxine.'* A medication given to those with hypothyroid problems.

"A reaction to medication? Anaphylaxis?" Ian suggested.

"No."

"I can't think of anything related to thyroid drugs? Apart from the exceedingly rare of course."

"Well, this is exceedingly rare- but luckily for him I have seen it a couple of times before. He is having a thyrotoxic crisis Ian, remember this for I'm sure it will be a long time before you see another one!"

"Right…" Ian thought this was so rare it probably did not exist, so to hear it was happening was altogether baffling! The diagnosis fixed Ian's mind and he wondered how Merlin had reached it. But he was used to consultants making random diagnoses, and now he mentioned it, it almost seemed obvious. All Ian really cared about was that Merlin was there taking control, and that he had not sedated the man.

"So what might precipitate this?" Merlin asked, taking the medical bag off Ian.

"Erm… overly aggressive thyroid treatment?" It was the only thing he could think of.

"Along the right lines. Recent thyroid surgery or radioiodine actually. He might also have had an infection, MI or trauma to the gland itself. How might we confirm that this is a thyroid problem?"

Ian had no idea. "Erm…"

"You must have some clue?" Merlin waited a few more seconds. "No? No matter. You would confirm with technetium uptake if possible but one should not wait for this as urgent treatment is needed. If you were in hospital you would ideally enlist expert help from an endocrinologist. Unfortunately you just have me, so I will tell you what you need to do."

Ian was not really used to being asked to actually treat patients, but he supposed he had to learn sometime.

"All the things you need are in here. But as with any patient, start at basic principles with Airway, Breathing and Circulation assessment. I don't think this patient is ill to that point and it is a lesson we will cover in more detail on your enrolment, so for now I want you to put a cannula in."

"I'm rubbish at putting cannulas in," Ian said like a reflex, as he did every time someone asked him to put a cannula in. The patient looked up at him as if he had just punched him in the face, clearly understanding that. "You have done one before successfully?" Merlin asked glancing over the top of his glasses.

"Well yes on the second attempt but-"

"Then you are not rubbish. Pick a vein in the anterior cubital fossa, easy. Draw some blood off at the same time please. The key is to believe you can succeed, and then you will. If you tell yourself you can't before you even try, then you will fail. Oh and don't get flustered by everyone else watching you. Just ignore them. They probably could not do it better themselves. Well perhaps I could, but don't mind me." Merlin grinned.

Ian sighed. He got his cannula ready, made the skin taught as an anaesthetist had recently told him was crucial, went for the vein- and missed. He swore under his breath and the patient winced. The wind howled outside, and the helicopter flew past the window. The weather seemed to be improving, if only slightly. On the second attempt the cannula slid into the vein beautifully. He drew off a syringe of blood, and then flushed it through.

"Good! Now give him Intravenous 0.9% saline, 500ml over 4 hours. If he was vomiting we could have put in an NG tube but he is not, so this is not necessary. Take blood for T3, T4 and cultures to check he has not got an infection. There is not a contraindication with this man so now give him propranolol, a beta blocker, to slow his heart rate. Got that?"

"Is this all in here?" Ian asked rummaging about sending medications left right and centre into one huge heap in the middle of the neatly arranged container. He fought to remember what Merlin was telling him.

"Yes, yes boy…Oh and high dose digoxin may be needed to slow the heart. Let's also consider giving him anti-thyroid drugs, Carbimazole. After 4 hours we must remember to give him Lugol's solution orally for 1 week to block his thyroid as well as Hydrocortisone or dexamethasone steroids. If I thought there was a suspected infection I would treat it with an antibiotic- perhaps cefuroxime. We would then follow him up by adjusting his IV fluids as necessary, cooling him with tepid sponging plus or minus some paracetamol. He'll also need follow up of course and doses adjusting. We can sort that out when we are back though." After spouting out all this information, Ian did not know if he was coming or going. Certainly this was exciting, but he certainly felt incompetent. "Tell you what, think he needs to come back with us for monitoring. Take him up to the helipad, and we will winch you both up. Unless the heli can land now."

The man had calmed down a lot now, but the weather had not, so Merlin and Ian attached the patient to the stretcher and the crew and staff helped get him ready to be sent up over the bitter cold seas of the north. After some trouble, Merlin was taken up first, and then the pilot lowered the winch. The crew who had much more experience of this sort of thing than Ian, attached it to him and the stretcher. He felt a lot calmer the second time round. The stretcher and he slowly waved goodbye to those below. Merlin got them into the helicopter, and slammed the door once the patient was secure. Ian noticed that having a patient to focus on made him not quite so scared. The chopper made its way back to Tynemouth and the man was unloaded and transferred onto an ambulance which was waiting.

Still high on his natural adrenaline, buzzing with excitement Ian followed Merlin down into Tynemouth priory's depths. This was it. His results. "Congratulations Ian Mellows, you have passed. I was pleased by the fact that although you are clearly not naturally brave, you managed to get over your fears and still pushed on through to get the job done. Excellent. Your training will start at a time of our choosing. A person from the service will make themselves known to you and you will be given orders in the form of a sealed envelope. Each of these you must then destroy." Ian's chest swelled with pride. He was asked there and then to swear an oath of allegiance to the queen called 'attestation' and initiate his training process into the secret service.

This was exactly the sort of organisation he wanted to be in. Full of pride for queen and country and feeling about ten feet tall, Ian wandered out of the priory. He could not wait for the next challenge, and felt happy again. It had been along time since he had felt happy about his career! He just wished he was not starting respiratory medicine next week, what a boring topic compared to oil rigs! Well at least it was not back to Mr Bing.

Chapter Five: Combat Medic Training

The following week, Ian came into medical school as if he was drunk. He had a secret that no-one else knew and it felt delicious. He was on edge. He found himself looking around at every dinner lady, every cleaner, every porter- as if they might at any moment whip out an envelope addressed to him with the words 'on her majesty's service,' at its top.

But for the first week of respiratory medicine, the letter did not come. It did not come in the second week either. He wondered if maybe he had in fact failed his first test, they had decided not to allow him to pursue the career after all. He turned to the depressed looking foundation one house officer he was shadowing, a girl called Jane. She had tiny freckles on her face, strawberry blonde hair, (not ginger she had reassured him,) and a harsh Irish accent. Every day he had seen her she looked as if she wanted to walk to the top of the east tower, and jump off it. Luckily she had not, for she was one of the nicer doctors he was shadowing, and at least seemed to care about how he was doing, about whether he was being ignored or not, and more importantly if there was nothing important to do would either send him home or to the library to do something useful with his time.

Her bleep went, and after a few depressed sounding, 'uh-huhs,' she replaced the phone, her face red with anger. "Sodding research department," she snorted. Ian had not seen her angry before.

"What's up?" he retorted.

"I've been sent a list as long as my arm of xrays I have to order through the online system. I have never met the patients before, but because I'm a doctor I have to order them. And I just know the radiographer will bug me about ordering them wrong- there is always something!"

"Do you want me to do it?" Ian asked.

"You don't have a password, its ok I'll get it done."

"Give me yours- come on you're busy enough without doing this monkey work- it'll give me something to do."

"It's all monkey work," she responded sullen faced. "It would help a lot though, if you're sure?" Ian nodded.

"Ok thanks that's such a help. I've got a lady with maleana on ward 2, and a man whose impossible to bleed on ward 4. Not to mention the woman on the LCP's family who want to speak to a doctor, even though I'll tell them nothing different from what the nurses have."

"Where are the other team members?" Ian asked innocently.

"On leave, or in clinic. I'm on my own." After a short introduction on to how to order the xrays, and a strict order to make sure there is an appropriate indication, (usually saying 'query infection' would get it done,) Ian felt very pleased with himself after bashing out thirty xrays. It was only when the phone rang next to him, that a surge of anger came over him. It was Mark, the radiographer. "Ian Mellows?"

"Yes? Hello," Ian said politely.

"I'm mark the chief radiographer. You have wasted my time ordering those xrays," the man said aggressively. "I mean you've filled it all out wrong- totally wrong."

"Oh sorry-"

"Sorry doesn't cut it mate- I mean it's just common sense isn't it."

"Ok well what have I filled out wrong?" Ian asked confusedly.

"You should know what you have filled out wrong. I'll be filling in an incident report form about this."

"Just tell me what I've filled out wrong?" Ian's blood was getting up- why did people in hospitals feel they could talk to you like such a lowlife?

"Well to start you've not written the xray required." Ian felt bemused.

"But I've filled out a chest xray form, therefore showing I need to order a chest xray?"

"You haven't written 'chest xray' in the clinical information box."

"But it's a chest xray form? I wouldn't want a hip xray if I'd ordered a chest xray would I?" Ian said obviously.

"Well you've not written an indication."

"I have I've written 'query infection' as an indication?"

"Yes you have but you haven't written which side."

"Ok...fine. Ill change it."

"And you need to write the code of the research project, and the name of the patient and their date of birth."

"But the code of the research project is in the box saying, what is the research project code?"

"Ah but you have to write it out again in the clinical information."

"But the patient's name is on the xray form- I order it under the patient's records- I would not order an xray for a woman on a different person's record? And the date of birth automatically prints on the form? Can you not see it or something your end?" Ian was bemused- what on earth was the problem? He hoped to god there was not this sort of bureaucratic nonsense in the secret service- if only he could tell this bloody imbecile! See him be rude to him then!

"I can see it, but it's not the way it's done. You have to write it all out again in the clinical information box." Ian sighed. This man was an obstructive arsehole, nothing would make him do the xrays unless Ian did what he said.

"Ok I'll change them," he said, defeated.

"Good. And in future sort this out. I've got enough things on without having my time wasted by people like you."

'Like drinking coffee and eating cake you fat bastard'- Ian thought to himself.

"And another thing. I've not met you. Make sure you get yourself up here and introduce yourself. You need to see what we do here to prevent things like this happening again."

"Will do," Ian said with no intention of following it up. Who the hell was he, the queen?

"Arrogant arse." Ian said to Jane half an hour later.

"Yep. Total chip on the shoulder. If I had a pound for every time I had a bleep from that team, I'd be a rich lady... Thanks for doing that. Anyhow, do you want to go to the library? I'll see you tomorrow, there's not much more to do here." Ian walked out of the ward still feeling frustrated. He wanted to have another go at that radiographer. But it probably was not worth it, it would not change anything.

As he walked along the respiratory ward outside corridor, he heard a voice from behind him calling his name. A secretarial looking lady approached him and handed him a letter. A buzz of adrenaline, and then a tremble in his bladder. This was it. He smiled excitedly. "Thanks," he said, but the woman was already walking off. He checked no-one was looking, and tore it open.

Get to the helipad. Ten minutes.

Merlin.

Ian ran to the nearest set of stairs, and belted up them. He used his special security card Mr Vesely had given him, and walked out onto the helipad. He was met by wind and rain- and another day of freedom from those clinical walls of hospitals. That was when he heard the helicopter blades beating against the clouds, steadily getting nearer. He smiled, and took a deep breath. "Finally," he said to himself.

This time it was a large military helicopter, which he later learned was called a 'Chinook.' It had two sets of rotary blades, one at the front and one over the tail and Ian could not work out how they did not crash with each other for they overlapped. The thunder was much deeper than the coast guard helicopter, and he felt the pressure deep in his chest as it landed. He had to crouch down for fear of falling over. Merlin was on board, and handed him a headset. Ian thought such a big helicopter was a bit of a waste as there was only one other man on it, dressed in army fatigues with a red cross on his arm. He wore dust glasses and had very short hair which was receding somewhat, the grey hairs of stress induced old age poking through. Merlin made the introductions shouting over the noise. "This is Jim! Captain Jim Reece! Your mentor whilst in the deployment phase of your training. A very experienced and respected anaesthetist with several tours of the middle east and Africa under his belt, learn as much as you can from him!" After introducing the two of them, Merlin bade him farewell and jumped out of the helicopter. "Got a meeting!" he shouted. He then marched nonchalantly across the helipad to the ramp which led down to the hospital. In the next moment he was gone. Ian felt very alone, but that did not matter, for they took off. He strapped himself in quickly, but felt a lot safer in such a sturdy looking aircraft.

Jim Reece was warm and smiled broadly, "Nice to meet you Ian! We're heading down to Catterick Garrison for some basic military training before you are unleashed upon the general population, and before your deployment! Just remember, you know much more than you think- and if you don't know something ask me. That ok?" Ian nodded.

An aching weight started at the bottom of his stomach and grew heavier, lurching from side to side as the chopper turned. Cold wind blew in his hair and after about an hour, they touched down amongst some tall, dark green hills. Jim led them off onto a wide open concrete area. There were military 'no entry' signs dotted about the place, and he spotted a notice which read, 'Warning: Unexploded Ordinance on this training area.'

'Well that's good to know'- he thought to himself. Jim led him over to a small, corrugated iron troop shelter at the edge of the square. The helicopter's blades slowed down as the pilot turned off the engine. The sound of birdsong eventually became more prominent than the robotic whirring. The silence was bliss. A huge, rocky hill, the biggest of all those around was in the distance towering over them, and Jim pointed at it. "That's Murton Fell. Do some of the mountain rescue training over that way." It sounded impressive to Ian, so he made a face of being impressed. Jim opened the door to the shelter, and they both walked inside.

There were several tables dotted about the area, with many different pieces of equipment on them, both military and medical. It was much warmer in here and felt as if a fire had been burning. Jim picked up a sleeveless jacket which was on the table. He threw it at Ian, who caught it. He then nearly dropped it. It was much heavier than it looked. "Put this on, may as well get used to wearing it now. It's heavy, and it's restricting. But by god if a grenade goes off anywhere near you it might just save you getting shrapnel in your back when you are in Iraq." He winked. Should he wink back? Ian pulled the body armour over his head. It was indeed heavy to wear. The thought of shrapnel in his back sent a shiver down his spine, and he did it up tightly. He then attempted to smile, but it came out as more of a grimace. He then registered what Jim had said- he was going to Iraq? Bloody hell.

"I would like to go through a whistle stop tour of trauma and managing the emergency patient. This is a war you are entering. Pressures are not only on you in saving the patient, but also from the environment which surrounds you. And the environment of Iraq is by no means as accommodating as this environment of Catterick and Murton fell. But at the same time, you may encounter things out in Iraq just as you will encounter here in Britain. It is the medic who misses those simple things by presuming it is something complicated as a result of the battlefield who will kick himself the most. At the same time- common things are common- and common things in battle are gunshot wounds and blast lung- not COPD," he paused and walked over to another table which had an array medical equipment on it. "Let's talk through a scenario. You are driving to London on the A1. Ahead of you is a car crash, you are a medical student. What do you do?"

Ian paused. What would he do? He was still taken aback by the thought of going to Iraq. Iraq? There were terrifyingly scary things happening there! "Err…" he smiled awkwardly. Jim did not return the smile. "Drive around and pretend it did not happen?" Ian laughed awkwardly.

"Where would you pull over?" Jim asked him ignoring the joke.

"Not sure, it is difficult to know. On the slip road?"

"You could, but how do you signal to the cars behind you there has been an accident?"

"Well- maybe across the lanes with your warning lights on?" Ian was guessing.

"Vaguely… You would angle your car across the lanes away from the other side of the carriageway."

"So they can still see your reflectors?"

"And?"

Ian blanked, "So it blocks both lanes?" Jim shook his head.

"So that if a car hits your car, it will not have its wheels aimed straight at you and the accident, or at the oncoming traffic and go straight into any of them causing a worse accident. It hopefully would send the car off into the side of the road. If you park about 50 metres away from the accident, this also gives you time to hear the collision and get out of the way. Clear?"

"Clear?" Ian responded. Made sense.

"Think of the mnemonic, 'DR ABC' for the civilian world. Dr stands for 'danger.' Is there any danger? Is it safe to approach the vehicle? Is it a lorry containing chemicals or harmful materials? If so, do not become a casualty yourself. You can be a hero in helping someone in trouble, but do not try to be a superhero. To be a superhero and be invincible to danger- despite what films might suggest- is impossible and will result in your death." Ian nodded. "Which is of no use to anyone, least of all you." Ian nodded harder.

"Now you have got to the vehicle, it is relatively safe. What next?"

"ABCs?"

"ABCs, yes- but hold the thought. What would you do if say, there were 4 casualties. Driver is wandering around happily, the front passenger is screaming, and the two passengers in the back are not making any noise at all, and are unresponsive."

"Triage?" Ian suggested.

"Yes. Good. Triage. From the French, 'to sort.' " He took a permanent marker from his jacket and held it up. "You would sort the casualties into an order of priority. Just as a triage nurse at the Emergency department sorts casualties into categories from urgent to less urgent. Category one- entirely drop what you are doing now or the patient will die urgent- down to category four, broken finger nail priority- they can wait some time to be seen. How would you triage them in this situation?"

"Errr…"

"It depends, is the correct answer. In a military scenario, we use the numbering from T1 to T4, and would clearly mark the casualty status by writing it on their foreheads. T4, means dead. T1, is a first priority casualty with impending death if not treated. T2 slightly less urgent but requires treatment within a certain time period and T3 is generally not so urgent."

"Right." Ian fought to remember all this. Would he actually put this into practice soon?

"So you have triaged the casualties by assessing their ABCs. Tell me about this?"

"Airway, breathing, circulation."

"Bit more than that Ian! Add on D, E and FG to the end of your ABC." He slapped Ian on the back hard, smiling. Ian had knew a bit about the' DEFG.' "Remember, we are in a civilian situation now."

"Airway- Establish an airway, for without one, the patient will quickly die," Ian spurted out.

"Good. How? " Jim asked.

"Head tilt and chin lift? Or Jaw thrust manoeuvres."

"Yes- all good- but remember with Airway to think of cervical spine- in a car accident or other traumatic incident the patient may well have injured their cervical spine. In anyone with injures above the clavicles, or decreased levels of consciousness, suspect a cervical spine injury. This must be isolated and immobilised by a hand on either side of the head, and when possible a semi-rigid collar with two sandbags secured on either side of the head until proven that there is no cervical spine injury from xrays and other imaging. But yes, good- and remember to check the mouth to see if there is an obstruction present before doing any of this. You would kick yourself if after trying all of the airway opening manoeuvres there was a very simply removed obstruction in the mouth. Good- now onto breathing."

"I would check the respiratory function."

"How?" Jim pressed.

"Look at the neck for tracheal deviation and symmetrical chest expansion."

"What else?"

"I would put my cheek to the patient's mouth to feel for breath and would look at the chest to see if it rises and falls. I would listen with my stethoscope for normal breath sounds."

"Good luck in a battle mate." Jim laughed. Ian continued, a little put off by the remark- he kept going from civilian to military- which one did Jim want him to talk about?

"I would also check there were no deformities of the chest, rib fractures, lacerations and so on- probably before auscultating."

"Yes- things such as flail chest for instance?" Ian stared blankly at Jim. What the hell was flail chest?

"You know what flail chest is Ian?"

"Well I think a while ago I heard..."

"Right. Ok." He paused for a moment and shook his head. Ian's cheeks flushed red. Was this something he should know about?

"Flail chest is a part of the chest wall that has no bony continuity with the rest of the thoracic cage as a result of a trauma. Think of it as if someone has bashed your rib cage with a baseball bat and knocked a small chunk out of the bones which is now held together merely by the surrounding soft tissues- not other ribs. The flail segment moves against the rhythm of the rest of the chest as it is no longer attached to the rest of the fastened bone- as in it moves in on inspiration and out on expiration."

"Ok." Ian nodded enthusiastically. He loved this sort of emergency medicine. Jim went on to demonstrate a bit more about flail chest and its treatment.

"So, flail chest aside- tell me how you would manage circulation- including how you would control bleeding."

"Pulse, blood pressure, respiratory rate, skin colour and capillary refill time. Hypotension after an injury should be assumed to be due to hypovolaemia until proven otherwise. During your initial triage, any severe bleeding points should be controlled by applying a sterile pressure dressing or a pneumatic splint. In the civilian world, tourniquets are not necessarily used as they can cause more problems than they are worth such as crush injuries and ischaemia. But here is what I will tell you now. In Iraq, you will use the military mnemonic, CABC. The first C, stands for Catastrophic haemorrhage. If you have someone bleeding out from a femoral artery, or any other major artery, you do not piss about. A tourniquet goes straight on. In this situation you will be operating under the theory of damage control- where prevention of the triad of death is imperative. Do you know what the triad of death is?"

Ian had not heard of the triad of death. Jim moved over to the whiteboard balanced against the edge of the tent wall, and began to squiggle a diagram.

"It is the fatal triad of hypothermia, acidosis and coagulopathy. In the past, we as healthcare professionals have sometimes done too much in trying to resuscitate patients and made the trauma patient worse. We have made them cold by giving them fluid which was not warmed, the fluid has diluted their blood which is full of clotting factors, meaning the patient bleeds more, and attempted to salvage limbs that have been unsalvageable leading to infection systemically, and an overwhelming inflammatory cascade which results in disseminated intravascular coagulopathy, and results in their death."

"That sounded fascinating to Ian. He had always been taught that if someone was bleeding with a low blood pressure- the priority was to fill them back up with fluids."

"Damage control resuscitation comprises of several theories- including that of permissive hypotension- not overloading a patient with fluids and stopping the bleeding. Allowing them to have low blood pressure and then stopping the bleeding and turning the tap off! Make the patient stable, by any means necessary. Do not fear the tourniquet in the battlefield. They may lose their limb, but you may just save their life." Ian must have looked rather confused at this last statement, for Jim quickly moved on.

"Lastly with C- circulation in your initial triage, make sure to suspect internal bleeding such as intra-abdominal or intra-thoracic bleeding. Fractured pelvis or fractured femurs also bleed a lot. Pelvic injuries can allow a patient to bleed to death quickly- so think about using a pelvic binder in these situations, they will not tamponade arterial bleeds but they will venous. The key to all of these injuries is get them to corrective surgery as fast as is possible. Next is disability. We are now getting on to things we might do after treating the severely wounded when we have a bit more time on our hands, perhaps back in hospital now.

"Ok. D- Disability. Rapid neurological assessment of the patient's level of consciousness. Use the AVPU scale- is the patient A- Alert, V- responsive to voice or verbal stimuli, P- only responsive to painful stimuli such as rubbing the sternum or putting pressure on the suprorbital nerve. Or lastly U- is the patient unresponsive.

Of course you can also use the Glasgow coma score for a more detailed assessment, which is out of 15. What can cause a decreased consciousness in a patient, amongst other things?"

"Well. Many things- cerebral injury, hypoxia and shock?"

"Anything else?"

"Errr..."

"Could be secondary to alcohol or drugs could it not?"

"Yes... Yes..."

"Ok. Lastly then, briefly talk about E- environment and exposure please."

"Well, completely undress the patient, perhaps cutting off clothes if it is necessary. Look over the entire surface of the skin for injuries. You should think about rolling the patient, making sure the cervical spine is protected. Perform a rectal examination. A trauma series of X-rays must also be taken here. These include a lateral C-spine, chest and pelvic X-rays. And an ECG should also be done. And finally," he smiled at Ian. "FG- Never forget to check glucose. You will, believe me, kick yourself if you have not ruled out this simply reversed cause of trouble. More unlikely in trauma patients, but a common cause of collapse without trauma. And talking of glucose, time for a cuppa and choccie biscuit don't you think?"

Ian nodded sternly, and Jim walked over to the edge of the room where a large thermos of tea stood. He began to pour. "Take your tea NATO or civvie mate?"

"Sorry?" Ian asked, thinking he had misheard.

"One sugar or two?"

'Weird military medics'- Ian thought to himself.

Chapter Six: COPD

After tea, and after Ian had asked some more slightly terrified questions over his deployment to Iraq, Ian and Jim went through some basic procedures Jim thought Ian would need for Iraq. Ian listened intently, knowing that a lot of this could be lifesaving. Jim showed him the interosseus gun which was used to put fluids into a person via their bones if IV access into a vein was not possible. He showed him on various dummies the insertion of chest drains and needles and how to correctly apply torniquets. They went through exactly where everything was stored in the Chinook, and where in turn he should store things in his personal equipment. He also learnt the Iraqi dialect Arabic or 'Ammiah' for 'hello', 'do you have any pain' and 'I am British, please help me.'

They sat down after a few hours once more and Jim wanted to pick Ian's brains over a chronic condition which often coincided with others in the UK and caused a lot of hospital admissions. Like the UK, people in Iraq also suffered from it, smoking being a highly taken up pastime there. "So Ian, what is the difference between asthma, and COPD?"

"I must admit I have never quite grasped this, they always seem to be pretty similar?"

"They are similar in that they both are to do with obstructions in a person's airways. COPD or chronic obstructive pulmonary disease, is a progressive disorder which is fixed or is only partially reversible. It only ever stays the same or gets worse. Asthma, on the other hand, is usually reversible, so by the use of various therapies and so on, can be treated and patients can return to a relatively normal function. This is of course not to say it is not a serious condition that can kill in certain circumstances." Ian nodded.

"So you know what causes COPD I take it?"

"Cigarette smoking? Though I think there is a smaller link to atmospheric pollutants from industry and so on."

"Do you know if it one can be genetically predisposed?" Jim asked.

"I do not think you can?"

"You think wrong. Alpha 1 anti-trypsin deficiency pre-disposes a person to early development of COPD. What is the pathology?"

"Well, smoking causes bronchial mucus gland hypertrophy and increased mucus production, leading to a productive cough. Degradation of lung tissue with dilatation of the distal airspaces (emphysema) occurs, leading to a loss of elastic recoil, hyperinflation, gas trapping and an increase in the work of breathing. CO2 levels rise in the blood, and the normal respiration drive due to carbon dioxide levels switches to an oxygen led drive.

"This is why people bang on about why you should not always give 100% oxygen to the patient with COPD, as giving them oxygen will take away their hypoxaemia and may lead to cessation of breathing. This is a very complex mechanism, best left to an anaesthetist. Remember that hypoxia will kill you, high CO2 will put you to sleep. Hypoxia kills first, so do not be too afraid to administer 100% oxygen, just make sure you monitor it very closely. This is why COPD patients get put onto Venturi masks, for they prevent too much oxygen being breathed by the patient in a safe manner."

Ian had heard many of these terms before, and whether it was due to lack of reading or what he did not know- but this seemed to be the first explanation which actually made sense to him.

"Anyhow. What are the clinical features of COPD? What does the patient present with?"

Ian thought back to his time in hospital, he had had little time to remember much about COPD. "Well," he paused. "Slowly progressing symptoms of cough and shortness of breath over several years in a smoker?"

"Yes- and how do we classify how severe it is?"

"I can't remember exactly- it's something to do with the degree of airflow obstruction on spirometry?"

"Yes- it is to do with the FEV1, or the Forced Expiratory volume over 1 second. Remember on spirometry there are several measurements- FEV1, FVC or forced vital capacity and the total lung capacity, as well as a few others." Ian remembered them just.

"What is cor pulmonale?"

"It is a right sided heart failure as a result of respiratory disease?"

"Yes- chronic infections in the lungs result in pulmonary hypertension leading to ischaemia and failure of the right side of the heart. So not only has the patient got difficulties with their lungs, but their heart begins to fail," he paused. "So what investigations would you do for COPD?"

"I suppose pulmonary function tests, chest xrays, CT scans and blood gases?"

"Yes, good. And how do you manage these patients?"

"Get them to stop smoking as priority- give them bronchodilators-"

"What bronchodilators?"

"Well, beta agonists such as salbutamol and salmeterol, and anti-cholinergics such as ipratropium bromide?"

"Good. Now tell me about respiratory failure?"

"There are two types- Type 1 and Type 2. Patients with type 1 respiratory failure are termed pink puffers as they look pink, thin and anxious breathing rapidly. In type 1, there is low PO2 in the blood, but no CO2 retention. I remember this as with Type 1, there is only one thing wrong with the blood gas. With type 2 respiratory failure there are two things- both low oxygen and high CO2 due to retention. With type 2 respiratory failure- the patients are described as being blue bloaters- they appear blue, bloated, large and quiet."

"Good summary Ian. Now what would you do in an acute exacerbation of COPD where a patient comes in critically ill?"

Ian had just been on a respiratory ward for two weeks, so COPD was clearly fresh in his mind. "Firstly I would employ an ABCDE approach. Moving on from this, treatments would need to be increased, antibiotics given to reduce purulent sputum and respiratory deterioration. Oral steroids do improve recovery from acute exacerbations. Long term inhaled steroids reduce the frequency of exacerbations of those with moderate to severe disease and should be used in those with an FEV1 of under 50% and at least one exacerbation per year. Pulmonary rehabilitation is also very important- and various surgeries could be considered for resecting large bullae or to attempt to improve the elastic recoil of the lungs via lung volume reduction surgery."

"Good. And finally what is the prognosis?" Jim seemed please so far. Ian did seem to be getting it all right!

"It varies. If the patient continues to smoke, lung function will deteriorate more rapidly. Long term oxygen therapy, I believe, is the only thing shown to improve life expectancy."

"Good. Good." He paused, sipping from his tea. "It seems you know this pretty well. Whether you can apply this knowledge to a real life situation is another matter though! Soon we will see I suppose. Good. This is just a brief chat through various tasks. The next phase of your training will be with real patients, and will be conducted by Dr Merlin back at the radar station at Tynemouth priory. You will be presented with a series of tasks involving patients, again at a time of our choosing. Go back to med school, and swat up on several chronic diseases. If you know them like you do COPD, you should have no problems. Focus mainly on what to do with an overdosed patient, a diabetic patient, and an epileptic. You know what Merlin is like, swat up as he likes to push you.

"Work hard, and the results will come to you. Next time I see you will be in a country a lot hotter than this. The Chinook will take you back to Newcastle, I'm staying here for an exercise with SOCA, the serious organised crime agency. Escape and evasion." Ian wondered if perhaps he should learn some of that. "Good luck and see you soon," and with that, Jim stood up, shook Ian's hand and walked out of the bunker. Ian then heard the whir of the Chinook engine, and realised his ride home was almost ready.

Chapter Seven: Ground hospital training

2 months until Iraq

Several weeks passed and Ian waited on tenterhooks to get the next call. He could not wait, and by now was working as hard as he had ever worked during medical school. Swatting up all night and day, every moment spare he had. Even Jane had noticed and said how he had seemed to have a 'boundless energy.' If only she knew, Ian thought. At present, on this rainy morning in Sunderland hospital- Ian and Jane were deep in an argument with a pharmacist. "But this is the second time this has happened and Mrs Ellis has been delayed from leaving hospital?" Jane was saying.

"Well you gave in the TTO pharmacy record far too late for it to be processed the first time, it's a dosset box you know. We need at least 24 hours. So that's not my fault." The pharmacist sneered back.

"But what is it now, why has there been another hold up?" Jane looked tired and pissed off. This conversation had clearly happened many times before. The fiery Spanish pharmacist continued.

"You have prescribed clopidogrel- with omeprazole. This is incorrect."

"No it is not- I want them to have a protein pump inhibitor (PPI) to reduce the risk of stomach ulcers due to the NSAID? This is very normal?"

"No but hospital policy, is that you prescribe lansoprazole with clopidogrel. Not omeprazole."

"But they are both PPIs, they do the same thing. If I change this, this will take you another day to redo it."

"Yes," the pharmacist was not budging.

"I don't mind the fact its omeprazole- in fact I want the patient to have omeprazole, that's what the consultant ordered so I won't go back on the order."

"It is my duty to say I am not comfortable with this, and I will have to call your boss."

"Call my boss then!" Jane said walking off. "Obstructive time wasters in this place," Jane uttered under her breath to Ian. Ian could not see what the problem was. "This has happened before, and this lady is elderly with a lot of co morbidities. She is a sitting duck for getting a chest infection, hospital acquired, which will kill her. Do these people not see that? Of course not- they don't see the patients, they just fill out forms and follow protocols. It's me that has to explain to the family that their relative who was simply waiting for a bedrail or a chair or a bit of medication in hospital has now gone from being right as rain, to a festering septic nearly-corpse, who has one more night to live. Drives me mad this place."

Ian felt for Jane, she looked emotionally exhausted. He gave her a hug, and she burst into tears in the doctor's office. He felt helpless. "Just for a different type of PPI! That's all! And I'll probably get reported for delaying the discharge." Ian said they'd go for a drink after hospital to cheer her up and take her mind off it.

Two days later, Jane was called to see Mrs Ellis who was waiting for her lansoprazole dosset box. She had spiked a temperature. Lo and behold, she was septic with a pneumonia. The consultant came to see her, and placed her on the care pathway for the dying. Jane had to explain this to Mrs Ellis's family, who were totally devastated. But worst of all- they were very understanding and praised Jane saying that she had done all she could. Jane once again left the hospital in tears.

The next letter came, before Ian had even reached hospital three days later. The lady in the local bakers where he used to buy his lunch had handed him a letter, and the usual surge of adrenaline entered him. He raced to the roof. The chopper, this time a Lynx, picked him up and dropped him on the helipad near Tynemouth priory- he was to go into it to meet Dr Merlin. Merlin greeted him with a bored smile and showed him a chair. He sat down nervously on the chair behind the desk. Merlin was smoking a pipe, and the smoke made the room misty. The blackboard had 'Poisoning' written on it in large, white letters. A projector shined a computer screen onto a white painted area of stone wall to the left of the blackboard. The room was dimly lit by lanterns and candles. The only electronic implements in the room were the computer and projector. "Here starts the ground phase of your training. Here at Tynemouth we have our very own clinic and operating rooms for training medical agents such as yourself. The next few training missions you will conduct will be from this clinic and operating base. The methods we use here are certainly not orthodox, but you will get used to them.

Dr Merlin clicked a button at the lectern and walked over to him lowering his glasses to the end of his nose. A video screen came onto the wall. It was of what appeared to be a CCTV camera attached to somebody at about waist height. They were walking towards a building. The camera stopped and focused on a sign reading, 'Red Farth Conference Centre.'

"Where is that?" Ian asked.

"No matter, Mellows. Your lesson today is on poisoning. The man carrying this camera is a trainee from MI5, who is also being trained as a ground operative. He is currently in the phase of being trained in the art of assassination via poisoning. He is carrying a substance to pour into one of the participant's orange squash. He is about to provide you with a patient who has taken an overdose."

"What?"

"Stop saying stupid monosyllabic words boy and get ready to think," Merlin said irritably. Ian sat still. Light flickered onto Merlin's face from the candles in a way which Ian thought made him look like a bit like Dracula. Staring at the screen, Ian simply watched. The man had now entered the conference and was at the reception. What was this?

"This is not right!" Ian exclaimed.

"It will be not right if you let the person he poisons die. Now start thinking. We all have to start somewhere." Ian began to sweat heavily. He could not back out. Or could he back out? Perhaps someone else would save him. Could he take that risk? Adrenaline filled him and his heart hummed nervously. The man had now entered into a dining room. Vast arrays of people in smart suits sat in twos and threes around quite wide, neatly decorated tables. The odd member of restaurant staff passed the camera's view holding a tray of drinks or canapés. Ian felt sick.

"What are the most common things which cause death by poisoning boy?"

Ian thought desperately. He now knew why swatting up on various conditions was so imperative- he only wondered what else was in store for him after this! Why had he not done this more thoroughly! "Erm- Paracetamol I'm sure that's one."

"Faster boy." The video now showed that the man had approached a table. Two elderly men sat at it calmly waiting for lunch. Ian could not hear sound but could see the person with the camera was talking to them as they slowly ate their food.

"Paracetamol- and antidepressants- yes the Tricyclics- I'm sure they are- and car exhaust fumes- carbon monoxide. I think that's another."

"One other please," Merlin remained as cool as a cucumber. It sickened Ian at how used to this he was. A wind blew at the entrance to the dungeon.

"I don't know."

"Co-Proxamol boy. It's a mix of Paracetamol and Dextropropoxyphene, an opioid analgesic. That's one for free. It was so commonly used in overdose that it is now no longer commonly prescribed." Ian had never even heard of the latter drug. Dextropropoxyphene. One to remember. The camera now showed the man pouring out some juice to both of the elderly men.

"A drug from the groups of drugs you have just mentioned, has just been poured into an elderly gentleman's drink. They will be brought here, and you will sort them out."

"But how? I have no idea where to begin..." He expected Merlin to say he was joking.

"Well start by telling me the methods of dealing with a poisoned patient. And hurry. Symptoms will begin to show soon."

Dr Merlin walked slowly to the blackboard and picked up a piece of chalk from the rung at its bottom. "Must I tell you everything boy?" Ian felt sick. He could not help but feel that the poor man who was about to be overdosed and suffer because of it was at the mercy of him and his uselessness. Why had he said he wanted to do this in the first place? The telephone rang.

"Just a minute boy."

Ian stared at the board frantically trying to remember what Merlin had told him. But how would he treat the man to be brought in? What if he gave him the wrong thing? What if he killed him? He began to shake. The thought had not entered his mind before, that he might kill someone by mistake. What if?

Merlin chatted on the phone in the background at the side of the room. Ian could not make out the full conversation. After a few responses and nods of agreement, Merlin hung up the phone. "He is fifteen minutes away. You appear to be lucky- it is a sixty five year old gentleman coming in. No significant past medical history. Member of the Lithuanian security services," he laughed to himself. Ian did not find it amusing.

"Fifteen minutes for you to learn all you need to know about treating the poisoned- we must work fast," he grinned casually. "Ok, a method for dealing with poisoning and overdose is what?"

"Get rid of the drug from the body somehow?"

"Precisely! How?"

"Not sure."

"Think!"

"Flush them through? If they don't vomit it then push it through the other way?"

"I'll give you it- enhance the elimination we call it- correct. Try to get rid of the drug from the body as fast as possible- faster than normal. Three methods. One is to simply give repeated doses of activated charcoal. This is relatively safe, and hopes to get rid of the drug through gastrointestinal dialysis. It is not commonly used though as results are spurious on whether it works. Good. Know any others?" He looked at him curiously. Ian could only think of the man who was on his way to them now.

"Erm."

"Alkaline diuresis and Haemodialysis or Haemoperfusion. To briefly describe- Alkaline diuresis involves making the patients urine alkaline to alter the way things are excreted and reabsorbed in the kidneys. Weak acids are ionized in the renal tubules of the kidneys, and reabsorption is lessened as a result of alkaline urine." This went over Ian's head. "Haemoperfusion and Haemodialysis are more tricky methods. A cannula is put into both an artery and a vein in an arm usually, in order that blood can be filtered through either activated charcoal, as in haemoperfusion, or through dialysis membrane and fluid, as in haemodialysis, so that the drug passes into these substances respectively and out of the blood. Got that?"

"No," Ian said abruptly.

"Well today you will be using neither technique so don't worry. But read up on them, they are important. Today is more simple. When the man comes in, I want you to work out what drug he has taken, and administer the correct antidote. Simple."

"But I don't know the anti-dotes!"

"Then let us go through some more boy."

Ian felt outraged by this guinea pig patient created for him, but nevertheless the duty to a poor man who was now probably ten minutes away kept him there. "What do I give in Paracetamol overdose?" he asked frantically.

"Let us start answering your question by looking at what causes death from paracetamol overdose."

"But I just need to know what treats it!" he interrupted impatiently.

"Enough boy- as soon as you start thinking this way you risk negligence. Yes it might work 100 times that you give an antidote without realising how it works. But the 101th time there might be another factor in the equation and administering the anti-dote will kill the patient." Ian sat still for a moment, and then tried to push Merlin on. He did not want a lecture.

"Paracetamol overdose makes your liver shut down. After a delay I think," Ian said.

"Good- after 48 to 72 hours. Go on."

"I think twenty tablets can kill you?"

"Yes roughly ten grams of the stuff. But how?"

Ian had definitely just read this before coming in today. "In high doses the liver converts paracetamol into quinone to try to get rid of it. Quinone has to be inactivated by Glutathione, but high doses of paracetamol use up all the stores of Glutathione in the liver, leading to the quinine running riot and binding to the thiol in the liver cell."

"Cell protein." Merlin interrupted.

"Yes- well when this happens, the cell dies as it can't function. The patient then dies of liver failure if enough cells are killed off."

"Good!" Merlin seemed genuinely happy and for a split moment so did Ian. He then remembered the overdosed man and began to shake again.

"Acetylcysteine, and less commonly used Methionine are lifesaving in the person who has taken an overdose of paracetamol because they increase the production of liver Glutathione. Though if the patient has taken too much, sometimes they are past the point of no return. Very good boy," he moved over to the black board and began to write this on the board. 'Paracetamol- Acetylcysteine and Methionine- potentially lifesaving.'

"Ok, tell me about Opioid overdose."

"You give intravenous Naloxone." Ian retorted, again he had just read this.

"Good. What are the symptoms of Opioid overdose?"

"Coma and respiratory problems?"

"Yes! Good. Pinpoint pupils, coma and respiratory depression are classic Opioid overdose symptoms.

Naloxone should be given in repeated doses until ventilation of the patient is adequate." He again noted this on the board.

"You have two left. Tricyclic antidepressant overdose, and aspirin overdose. What do you know?" Ian definitely knew nothing of these, he remembered a vague fact about the tricyclic treatment, but nothing more. A buzzer went at the side of the room. Ian looked at the projector and saw the side of an ambulance, a patient on a stretcher, and the outside of the ruined priory which they were underneath. The patient had arrived.

"Looks like you have run out of time. This will have to be on the job training boy."

Ian gulped and followed Dr Merlin through the chamber and into the mock up hospital ward room. "Still waiting on the Tricyclics and Aspirin boy," Merlin said as if taunting him. He washed his hands and put on some rubber gloves. The patient was breathing slowly, and was shouting things. Luckily he was not in coma.

"So aspirin? What would the patient be displaying?" Merlin asked.

"Well, tinnitus, hyperventilation and sweating."

"Is he doing this?"

"No."

"How can you tell?" Ian walked over to the poor man and asked him what was wrong. The man flailed about on the bed and made no sense. He looked terrified.

"I cannot if I am honest."

"Good. Perhaps you would like to send his blood off to check for levels of any suspicious drugs? A toxicology screen as we might call it?"

"Yes ok." Ian succeeded in getting a cannula in the ante-cubital fossae, and took some blood.

"Bearing in mind he has been poisoned, how are you going to manage him?"

"Well I will need to know what the drug is first before I can treat."

"No- first you will maintain his airway, breathing and circulation will you not?"

"Yes, yes of course." Ian thought that was obvious.

"Good. Do you think if this was paracetamol overdose he would be displaying symptoms yet?"

"No... No... paracetamol would probably only show the effects after 48 hours."

"Good. So, we will test for this in the blood as a routine, but it is unlikely with such a short history. And would you expect his breathing to be depressed with aspirin overdose?"

"No."

"So we might rule that out possibly?"

"Yes, unless the bloods say otherwise."

"Good. So out of what we have discussed, what are we pointing towards here Mr Mellows?"

"Opiod overdose?"

"Have you checked his pupils? Are they pinpointed? Is his breathing depressed? What is his respiratory rate?"

Ian quickly checked. "They are not, and his resp rate is fairly normal at about twenty a minute."

"Well, about twenty, is not exactly twenty. But yes you are right. I think you are correct to factor opioids into the equation as I would say the diagnosis s between opioid overdose and tricyclic overdose can be difficult to interpret. So will you administer Naloxone to counteract the opiod?"

"Err..."

"Or perhaps you would agree his picture fits more of a tricyclic poisoning? Anticholinergic effects result in toxicity, where one gets respiratory depression, hallucinations and convulsions. Most patients require only simple observation or supportive measures such as oxygen- in fact pass me the oxygen mask would you. They may develop arrhythmias such as sinus tachycardia as a result of the atropine like effect. Lengthening of the QRS complex is a bad sign and may precede convulsions. We can treat these arrhythmias with intravenous sodium bicarbonate. Clear?"

"Yes. So will we administer Naloxone?" Ian asked frantically. What did he have to do to save the man?"

"I probably would if I did not know the cause, it does no harm. Beware on giving too much naloxone to a patient who has been given an opioid such as morphine for pain- as if you counteract all of their pain medication they will start wailing in agony as their broken leg starts to hurt again!" He laughed. Ian felt like telling him to shut up.

"Good. Well I will tell you Mellows that you may stop your worrying, for the man has been given a toxic, but only slightly toxic dose of tricyclic and therefore will only require observation- despite the scene he is causing. Now go and get some lunch, and after lunch I will teach you about the next chronic disease- epilepsy. And boy- you need to work on the way you handle stress- it is a massive part of being a doctor, panicking gets you nowhere. And certainly not when you are in a warzone."

Ian took that last comment on board for Merlin was right, but shaken, pissed off and generally down about the way he had just been taught, Ian trudged out of the room to get a sandwich across the road at the Rocksalt Café. Was this any better than med school?

Chapter Eight: A Fitting Beach

After lunch, Ian felt slightly better. He was still apprehensive though- he had taken on board what Merlin had said about panicking- it definitely did not get you anywhere. And he had considered that really, this may have been rubbish not knowing much- but being a doctor in the secret service was truly much more appealing than being a doctor in a hospital. When he walked into the lecture room, Merlin was smiling. Ian's skin crawled with anxiety and completely forgot what he had just been telling himself. Merlin said for him to follow on, they were going to go outside for the next lesson.

    They reached the bottom of a very long stone stair case in which the sound of dripping water echoed up and down off the stone walls. They had reached a thick steel door, which was rusted. Merlin pulled the handle down with a loud clank, and pushed. Cold air rushed in, and Merlin led outside. The sound of waves crashing against rocks hit them as they stepped out onto sand which crunched underfoot. Merlin turned and looked at Ian. Facing him, were 6 equally spaced out people. They all were sitting on chairs, a couple on top of what looked like gym mats. Ian stood bemused, he could not work out what on earth this test was. Merlin grinned at him.

"This lesson is on epilepsy. You have done your reading?" Ian nodded, hoping to God he had done enough. Hoping that if, like the last test, someone's life was put in danger, he might know enough to save them.

"Good. Do not ask me how we do this, you might find that out if you manage to qualify from this medical school, but as I have told you- we have methods far more advanced than the normal realms of medical advance." Ian could not work out what he was getting at. Merlin pointed at a table to the right hand side of them. "You will notice, that on that table there are 5 medications, each of the correct dose. Each medicine must be administered to the correct patient who requires it, in order to treat their type of epilepsy.

"So I'll take a history from each of them first?" Ian surveyed the six, quietly sitting and watching. They all looked at him slightly strangely. A young girl smiled at him, he smiled back. A middle aged woman sat worriedly. A middle aged man sat stern faced. Ian noticed that all of them had electrodes strapped to their heads. The wires from these each ran into large boxes which looked like ECG machines.

Merlin shook his head. "No histories. You will be able to diagnose them from the type of seizure they display." He smiled widely.

"How can I tell that?"

"The how is what you might find out if you graduate from here. All you need to know now, is this." He took a mobile phone from his pocket and dialled a number. After a moment he said, "We are ready, ECTs connected."

Suddenly, all six patients dropped to the floor. The woman was convulsing violently, and foaming at the mouth. The man was smacking his lips together, pretending to smoke a cigarette over and over and over. The young girl sat totally glazed over, no longer smiling, simply looking. Another teenaged boy's arm was shaking and shaking. The most disturbing was a man who lay on the gym mat, and was convulsing very violently, shouting and screaming in no particular pattern at all.

"Fits lasting longer than half an hour fit into the category of status epilepiticus. If a fit lasts longer than a few minutes- you really want to start thinking about stopping it. Every second the fit goes on, the risk of hypoxaemia and irreversible brain damage is increased. Tell me quickly Ian what the fit is so that I can stop it. Hurry!"

"Can't you just stop them now?! I have seen the fits now, I'll remember them!"

"No, no. That would not be the way of the secret doctors. Now tell me what the fits are!" Ian thought back hard to his reading.

He spotted the child immediately, staring into nothingness. Really, the little girl looked to be bored and day dreaming. Ian waved his hands in front of her eyes. She did not respond. "She is having a typical childhood absence seizure!" The girl suddenly snapped out of it, and began to cry. Merlin sent her off to 'find her mummy' at a side door around the corner. "Good! That was rather a fast one- and what is the classical appearance on an ECG?" Merlin asked.

"Spikes and waves of 3Hz!"

"Good- used to be called petit-mal seizures, and can be provoked by hyperventilation. Medication to treat her?"

"Sodium Valproate or ethosuximide, but it's likely to remit by adolescence."

"Good! Next!"

They moved on to the man who was violently screaming and shaking all over the place. "No! Move to the woman, he can wait."

"Really?" Ian said concerned.

"Yes... The woman, Ian."

The blonde woman was still foaming at the mouth and appeared to be having a tonic-clonic seizure. She had initially had a brief tonic stiffening of the limbs with a sudden loss of consciousness followed by what was now clonic jerking.

"Primary generalized epilepsy." Ian said.

"Good. Treatment?"

"Sodium Valproate again?"

"Yes, good. Also responsive to Lamotrigine, which is also the drug of choice in pregnancy. Note that carbamazapine can make these seizures worse." He paused. "So what are we going to do to stop this fit? I mean, how long has it been going on for?"

"I-" Ian had no clue. He was still worrying about the others that were fitting.

"Exactly- make sure you start to time a fit as soon as you see it, it is very difficult to work out how long it has been going on for with hindsight. Take note of your watch hand as one of the first things you do when managing a seizure." Ian nodded.

"First of course, we would need to be sure of the cause of fit. Make sure you rule out things like hypoglycaemia, or eclampsia- is the patient pregnant? You would perform an urgent glucose, electrolytes and toxicology screen. You would also manage airway, breathing and circulation. But well as basic life support- she has a cannula in- what are you going to put through it to stop the seizure, bearing in mind this is quite a clear tonic-clonic epileptic fit? Usually they will run their course, and all you can do is ensure that the person does not hurt themselves, but if they do not stop after some minutes?" Merlin's calm and matter of fact manner, made Ian calmer, but he could still not help wanting to get on as the man flailed hither and thither on the mat next to him.

"Hmmm- Diazepam?" Ian ejected.

"Vaguely boy- more specific. Right area of drugs?" Ian looked bemused. "We use benzodiazepines." He winked. Ian wished he would hurry up. "For status epilepticus in adults we start with Lorazepam, 4mg as a slow bolus over 2 minutes into a large vein. We must be aware of the risk of respiratory arrest during the last part of the injection. As you can see," he pointed at a table with a defibrillator and crash call kit on it, "we must have full resuscitation facilities available for IV benzodiazepine use. We could also give rectal diazepam if IV access was difficult or buccal Midazolam as an oral alternative.

Beware that the doses for all of these drugs differ amongst different ages of adults and children respectively. With Midazolam, you squirt half the volume between the lower gum and the cheek on both sides. Why don't you try it." Merlin drew up the correct dose of Midazolam into a syringe and Ian went and knelt by the woman. With difficulty he did as he said. He squirted half of the syringe into one side, and half into the other. The woman stopped fitting. Merlin called someone on his phone and immediately, four men dressed in dark suits came from the side door and put her onto a stretcher, carrying her off into the depths of the medical school. "Next!" Merlin uttered. Ian's head was a whirlwind.

They ran to the mat with the teenaged boy on it. He was still sitting in his chair. His face had initially started with a rhythmical twitching, but this twitching had moved down through his arms and legs in a march-like fashion. "Jacksonian seizure or a simple partial seizure." Ian said immediately. "Good! The march like fashion of this seizure is as a result of the electrical activity spreading from the sensory cortex over the motor cortex of the brain." Merlin retorted. "I think he is coming to the end of the seizure." Merlin said, and within seconds the boy had begun to sit totally still again. It looked odd. "It is likely he will have a post-ictal loss of motor function for a few hours or over the rest of the day called Todd's paresis. Luckily we pay him well so he won't mind!" Ian went over to the man, who was not fitting quite so violently but still looked very worrying. "No, not yet." Merlin said. See this man first. He pointed at the man who had sat looking blank smacking his lips together. He now however, was not dong anything he simply sat looking dead ahead. Ian knew exactly what this was, for he struggled to understand how the fits worked. "This was a complex partial seizure." Ian said.

"Yes, good." Said Merlin. "These are common seizures, and usually arise from the temporal lobes." Ian wanted to get to the last man who still shouted out, but Merlin refused. "Tell us what you feel like when you get one of these seizures Harris."

"Well." The man had a gruff voice and a thick Geordie accent. "I get this like feeling that I have never experienced what I am doing, like I have never been in this situation before- and a funny taste in my mouth, like burnt rubber or something. Then I can't really remember anything. Like I can't remember what has just happened, I just know from previous times that this is what happens."

"Thank you Harris, you may go."

"Cheers Doc." Harris replied, walking off to the side door and away from the stiff sea breeze which had got up. "Right, and finally on to the one which looks the worst I think you might think."

Ian went to try to wake the man, he must have been fitting for at least ten minutes now. He had a cannula in. "We need to stop this sir?" Ian asked bewildered. Did Merlin not like the patient or something?

"Ok. Here is some Lorazepam. Start the infusion." Ian did not really know what to do so Merlin helped him somewhat. As they touched the man, the seizure got worse- he kicked more violently, and shouted at them, "Its getting worse! Its getting worse!"

The infusion went in, and Ian could not handle the nerves anymore. "What sort of fit is this?" Merlin asked him.

"I have no idea, it has no pattern at all- but it looks terrible!" The lorazepam had all gone in now, but still the man continued to fit if not in a slightly subdued way.

"Ok, well before tell you- the next step would be to put in a Phenytoin infusion, 15mg per kg at a rate of less than or equal to 50mg per minute. Don't whatever you do put diazepam in the same line, they do not mix. Beware of a decreased blood pressure when you do this, and do not use if the patient has a slow heart rate or heart block. It requires ECG monitoring and BP monitoring. 100mg over 6-8 hours s a maintenance dose."

"Ok." Merlin drew up the necessary, and administered it. But after still more minutes, the fit continued. Again, if not slightly more subdued.

"He is still not stopping!" Ian shouted.

"Ok, the next step is a diazepam infusion of 100mg in 500 ml of 5% dextrose. We infuse at about 40ml per hour, or 3mg per kg over 24 hours. Close monitoring now, is vital." They had applied all of the leads of the ECG and Ian took regular blood pressures. But the man continued to fit. Was he gong to have brain damage at the end of this?

"What do we do?!" Ian asked imploringly.

"Well, if we suspected a vasculitis or cerebral oedema from a tumour is possible we would give dexamethasone, a steroid. And if not, the patient would require to be managed in intensive care and put under general anaesthesia." Ian raised his eyebrows. Had the secret doctors made this man require intensive care?!

"But I believe none of these things to be necessary. The steps we have done in fact have not been necessary. It is very rare after an infusion of Loraepam, phenytoin and diazepam for a ft to continue. We must therefore consider a pseudo-seizure or non-epileptic attack disorder." Merlin walked over to the man, knelt down beside him, and said, "ok Mark, thanks- you can stop now."

The man who had worried Ian so much, who he had been terrified about, stopped fitting on command. He lay, looking chilled out from all of the drugs Ian had just given him. "we'll keep you monitored for the rest of the day until the drugs wear off ok?"

Mark nodded.

"What Mark has is termed non-epileptic attack disorder. This requires a referral to psychiatry, for the patient is trying to act as if they have epilepsy for one reason or another. Many of them can actually have epilepsy, and find that they crave the attention they receive after having a fit. Suspect these in people who show pelvic thrusts, resist attempts to open lids and attempts to do passive movements as well as a general abnormal pattern which does not fit into any category of fit. Any questions?"

Ian sat down on the floor baffled. He had never suspected someone might be putting the fit on! And he had just blasted this Mark full of drugs.

"Right, good days work Mellows. Straight here tomorrow morning, we'll send a car for you." And Merlin marched off the beach and up into the medical school. Ian lay back, and allowed the sound of the waves to overpower him, sending him into an exhausted sleep where he dreamt about a time when he did not study medicine, and oh how it was bliss.

Chapter Nine: The Diabetic Tramp

The chauffeur picked up Ian bright and early, and yet again he found himself wandering through the doors to Tynemouth priory to see Merlin standing by the lectern. He had not slept well, thinking about the two lessons he had earlier, and the fact he probably, was to get something worse today. Merlin, did not bat an eye lid at Ian's heavy eyelids or unkempt looks and wasted no time getting straight into it.

"Tell me about diabetes." Dr Merlin asked as he fiddled about with some keys on the laptop at the lectern. Ian sat up straight as the projector turned on. Was there another test coming? A stench of wet grass had filled the room, and beams of soft sunlight now shone in from outside the dungeon window. Beads of perspiration hung on Ian's forehead, and he gripped his hand firmly to stop it twitching. Dr Merlin's eyes searched him inquisitively.

"There are two types."

"Obviously," Merlin stared at him. "Anything more?"

"Type 1 and type 2."

"The difference being?" Merlin sarcastically asked.

"Type 1 presents early, and is an autoimmune disease. Type 2 is usually later onset and is characterized by insulin resistance and impaired secretion of insulin."

"Good. Which cells in the pancreas?"

"Beta cells."

"Good." Merlin continued typing on the laptop and a video screen came up on the area of white wall Ian had come to fear. "Good." A picture flashed up on it. A man sat in the middle of an empty room. Ian could tell it was somewhere else in the building by the way the bricks sat against each other. His heart began to thump. Please not another test? Dr Merlin picked up a small microphone from behind the lectern. "Hello David, you ok in there?" The man sitting on the chair said nothing.

"Bugger, sounds not on." He walked over to the lectern and pushed a button. "David! You ok there?"

"Yes, how much longer sir?" The man replied. He was dishevelled, had long dark hair and an unkempt beard which touched upon a dark coat.

"Not long, Mr Mellows is just getting ready to begin."

"Ok...When will I be getting paid? Same as last year?" The picture was not very good, but Ian could see the man was agitated.

"As soon as you wake up again. Don't worry, you'll be in good hands. Our man will be in soon. You signed the official secrets act didn't you?" Dr Merlin smiled.

"Yes I did." The man sat still and said nothing else.

"Good." Dr Merlin handed Ian an earpiece. "Put this in and check it works."

"What is this?"

"This is your next test. I'll explain in a moment. I hope you have done your memorising well." Ian switched on the small, grey earpiece and fixed it into his right ear. Merlin whispered into the microphone and Ian heard his voice loudly in his right ear. His breathing was fast. His mind raced, trying to work out what he was going to have to do.

"Soon I am going to ask you to walk into a corridor. The corridor has a series of doors in between you, and the room you see on this video screen." Ian stood looking bemused. He wiped his forehead of sweat.

"In order for these doors to open, you must answer some questions the director is going to ask you, correctly.

Once they are all open, you will reach David, and you can go about treating him."

"But there is nothing wrong with him."

"Mr MI5, please continue. See you soon David." Merlin spoke into the microphone clearly. "Watch this screen."

The man on the chair put his thumb up. This was bizarre! Then Ian's blood ran cold. He saw a man, dressed in dark glasses and a dark suit walk into the room. He held a syringe and immediately on entering the room injected the man David, with whatever it was that was in it. David sat still, nothing happened in the first few seconds. He then began to look drowsy. Ian focused on Merlin.

"What must I do?" He asked, wide eyed.

"David has Type 1 diabetes, and has just been injected with a very high dose of insulin. Such a high dose, that he is soon to enter into serious hypoglycaemia." Taking one last glance at the video screen, the man still sitting in the chair, Ian was shown through a door which closed behind him.

"Hurry!" Ian shouted. His mind focused- he had to get to the man quickly. He would not have this on his conscience. On the back of the door in front of him, was a small computer screen. It looked odd amongst the ancient ruin like effect of the priory's architecture. A question popped up on the screen. Merlin's voice filled the small compartment Ian now stood in. "It is touch screen Ian. Now hurry please, David will enter into coma shortly."

"Okay! I get it!" Ian shouted back.

"Keep your cool boy! The more you panic the less chance the patient has. What did I tell you before!" The screen flashed and a question appeared. *What level of fasting plasma glucose suggests a diagnosis of diabetes?* Ian knew the answer before the choices came up. He slammed his finger against the screen- 'OVER THAN OR EQUAL TO 7.0.'

Immediately, the door opened, and an equally sized compartment opened up, with another screen on the back of the next door. Ian pushed at it to check it really was locked. *True or False: Type 1 Diabetes Mellitus presents usually in younger people, is rare and is caused by autoimmune destruction of the Beta cells of the Pancreas. Type 2 has a strong genetic predisposition, is more common than type 1 presenting in middle aged to older people and is generally a result of resistance to the peripheral action of insulin.* Again, Ian knew the answer. If the questions continued like this, he would be in to the chamber before Merlin knew what had hit him. He slammed onto the screen, 'true.'

The door swung open. Another steel door was revealed barring his way- another screen bearing the key question on the back of it. *True or False: Oral hypoglycaemic agents are indicated in type 2 diabetes if diet alone does not control the disease well enough. Sulphonylureas such as gliclazide increase insulin release from beta cells. Biguanides such as metformin reduce insulin resistance and hepatic gluconeogenesis.*

Ian read and re-read the question. These were not exactly taxing, he wondered what the catch was? True! He pushed on the screen. The door swung open. "Hurry Ian." Merlin's voice rang out. *True or False: Glycated Haemoglobin or HbA1C is a good long term measure of glycaemic control?*

"True!" He shouted frustrated, this was a mickey mouse style test! But yet another door opened, to reveal yet another question. *True or False: The three domains of the Glasgow coma scale are: Best motor response, Best verbal response, Eye opening?*

"True!" Again Ian answered the buzzer. And now a different style of door was opened up in front of him, a glass door through which he could see a room with the man David laying in front of him, unconscious. Was he breathing? What should he do? "ABCDE" He said to himself. Then he saw the final question. This is perhaps why the others had been so easy. *What is this man's*

Glasgow coma scale score? Ian thought back, he knew there were three domains, but could not for the life of him remember how many points scored for each one.

"Errr! I don't know! I don't know!!" Ian screamed at the top of his lungs. The screen stared at him. He would fail. The man would die. He became panicked. He pushed at the glass door to try to open it. He hit at it. He hit at it again. Still it did not open. And then, from the ceiling somewhere dropped a scrap piece of paper attached to a bag of small pebbles which hit him on the shoulder. Ian swore and then picked it up. It had written on it the Glasgow coma scale.

Best Motor response: 6, orientated, 5 localizes to pain, 4 withdraws but does not localize to pain. 3 flexor response to pain, 2, extensor response to pain, 1 no motor response. Voice: 5- Orientated, 4 confused speech. 3- makes inappropriate speech 2-incomprehensible noises, 1- No sounds. Eye opening: 4- Opens eyes spontaneously, 3- opens eyes to voice. 2- opens eyes to pain. 1- no eye opening.

Ian looked at the man. A trap door opened in the glass door, and Ian realised what the pebbles were for. He picked one out and threw it at the man's abdomen. It was not something he would have done normally to an unconscious patient, but this was the only way he could save him! The pebble missed. Ian swore again, and threw another. It hit him on the side of his leg. The man made an odd spluttering noise, and his hand went towards his leg. He did not open his eyes. Ian judged he had a Glasgow coma scale score or GCS of 8, as he localized to pain, made an incomprehensible sound to pain, but did not open his eyes. He typed it onto the key pad. The door swung open. He ran over to the patient, automatically going to examine his airway. It was patent, and he was breathing

"What do I do?!" He shouted at no-one.

"Follow your ABCDE's Ian, you know that. Get a cannula into his antecubital fossae if his airway and breathing seem fine." Ian inserted one first time. "You need to give him IV 50ml of 50% glucose into his vein. You could also give intramuscular glucagon. We know the cause of this Ian, so no investigations are really necessary- but remember if this was a normal patient, look at how it might be difficult to ascertain what this man's cause of coma is- ABCDEFG- the FG being for never forget glucose!

"If you did not think a person was on insulin therapy or a sulphonylurea for instance, one might check insulin levels and C-peptide to rule out an insulinoma. There are also other tests to rule out the other rare causes such as addison's disease or IGF-II producing tumours."

"Right- what else do I need to do with him?" Ian did not care too much about the causes of hypoglycaemia, he just wanted this poor man to wake up.

"Good. That should be it my boy, pretty simple. Set up a drip for him would you, he'll just need a bit of monitoring now, perhaps with the odd tweak here and there if his sugar dropped again. This was a simple test Ian, do not forget it. Simple to show you that under pressure, the most simple of tasks can become impossible if you allow them to. But you reacted well. Good. I am pleased. Take him through, our agents from will help you. I will see you at our next lesson, I have a meeting to attend. Oh and one last thing- if this was the opposite and a hyperglycaemic state such as diabetic ketoacidosis- make sure you bring the man's blood sugar down slowly with fluids and Insulin infusions- doing it too fast can be very, very dangerous." And before Ian could say good bye Merlin had left to board a helicopter outside. The two men were putting the revived man onto a stretcher, and he was now much more awake. Before he went into the next room, he heard the man ask the man in a suit something, who responded by pulling a large wad of fifty pound notes out of his pocket and inserting them into the man's trousers.

Chapter Ten: Terrorist

Ian popped over to the Rocksalt Café again, and tucked into a bacon sandwich. The pretty waitress gave him a look of what Ian wondered to be interest, but he was so tired that he carried on eating, focused on what might be thrown up next. He was to meet Merlin back at Tynemouth at 14.00hrs that afternoon so had some time to kill. Maybe he could chat her up a bit later. He got out his notes, and started reading up on everything and anything he could- play it hard to get. He slowly was feeling more adjusted to these harsh throws into difficult situations as he got more used to them and to Merlin, and although he did not admit it to himself, he was starting to enjoy it. The adrenaline that went with it, certainly was addictive. "Hi there. I'm Ian," he said nonchalantly to the brunette as she cleared his plates. "Kate." She replied with a flick of her hair. "That looks like heavy work?" She remarked with a thick Geordie accent. She had deep brown eyes, and a short denim skirt sat on a very well toned body. Ian thought it would be too wild to ask her on date, he did not normally do that sort of thing. "Only university work," he said modestly. And then, because he was feeling wild he followed up with, "what time do you get off?"

"5." She replied with an intrigued smile, and a blush knowing what was to follow.

"Fancy a drink?" She smiled even wider and jotted her phone number of a serviette. Ian could not believe it, Merlin's madness must be rubbing off on him!

14.00 hours came, and Ian sat on the edge of his seat. Merlin began. "So, as you part of our duties as doctors in the secret service, we must provide skills to our government that perhaps would not be normally used in a hospital setting. You may be required often fulfil various duties in the pursuit of protecting the realm, and mop up the pieces after our comrades in the other more aggressive sects have done their work. Merlin lowered his spectacles to the end of his nose and sat down. He, as was now usual, pulled his pipe from his pocket and begun preparing it to light. Ian watched fascinated. An old fashioned thing it was to smoke a pipe, (and in his opinion foolish whilst knowing the terrible effects of smoking,) but nevertheless it was fascinating, and he hated to admit it something he respected. Merlin continued leaning back in his chair. We are also given aids to our teaching here in the form of patients whom our government would be quite happy to see 'get lost'." He paused, a small smile coming from the corner of his mouth. "Follow me won't you."

Merlin led him down into the depths of the priory, and to a room he had been in before, mirroring an intensive care ward Ian had seen at other hospitals. Monitors and wires and oxygen tanks and drugs cabinets lined the room, and there was a bed in the middle of it. On the bed lay an unconscious man. He had restraints around his arms. Monitoring was attached to him and he had various drips coming from various orifices. Were they about to perform an operation? "In front of you is a man called Viktor Franzech. Russian. He is known by most governments in the world to be responsible for funding terrorism. But his most famous success was when he singlehandedly murdered eight families, men, women and children- distant relatives of those who owed him money. He tortured them before he killed them."

Ian looked at the man on the bed calmly asleep. He had several scars across his lower neck and chest. What a despicable excuse for a human being! Ian hated him, even though he had not ever met him. Ian then saw a curious thing, what looked like an infusion line leading out from one of the veins in the prisoners leg. "What is happening to him?" Ian announced immediately. Several hours ago, this man was injected by our trainee learning to assassinate people- with a bacteria from the streptococcus groups. He is now, as you can see by the monitor going into septic shock. Our network has put Viktor forward for 'softening'. Meaning- he needs to be weakened in order for them to interrogate him effectively." Ian was not sure what he thought of this. To be a doctor was for good not harm- but then he had joined this organisation knowing what he was to let himself in for- the oath had suggested there might be occasions where to perform harm was a necessity. And this man was despicable! "What are we going to do? How do we know how far to push this? I mean this could kill him?" Ian asked like an inquisitive child.

"Yes so we must be careful Ian! We are going to just stop him going into renal failure. He has just lost enough to make him very weak, now we bring him round before it is too late… So on htat note- Acute Renal Failure- tell me the causes before we start?"

Ian was not sure at all what he thought of this. He wondered who had been involved and just left him. "Pre-renal, renal and post-renal." Ian blurted out like a sheep as was now the norm, putting these uncomfortable thoughts to the back of his mind and focusing on the casualty.

"Explain this slightly more please. As in- what does 'pre-renal' mean?"

"Well, pre-renal, as in, the cause is something systemic which causes the kidney to cease functioning properly- a kidney needs adequate blood flow, therefore if blood flow is reduced enough the kidney will fail. If a patient has a severe sepsis this can lead to renal failure and so on. If a patient is too dehydrated, this can also lead to kidney failure."

"Yes good. Good. This is how we are causing this man to go into renal failure, and hence why we have fluids ready to counter act the effect." Merlin smiled. As he mused on this further, the patient Viktor still lay unconscious. A shiver went down Ian's spine, but a lot less of a shiver than would have occurred before he had started this training. Ian did not realise, but he was becoming accustomed to the secret doctors way of doing things.

"It seems so." Merlin walked over to the bed. "You are right. Hypoperfusion or lack of blood flow around the body due to say, haemorrhage, will cause renal failure. As will sepsis due to infection. As will cardiogenic things, such as an acute coronary syndrome meaning blood is not pumped to the kidneys effectively. That is not to mention various drugs which can be the cause of pre-renal failure such as ACE inhibitors and NSAIDs. You can also get a hepato-renal syndrome where severe liver disease leads to renal failure." Ian nodded as Merlin ran his finger over the IV infusion which was dripping into the criminal in front of them. Merlin continued with his teaching. "The most likely histological result of pre-renal failure is acute tubular necrosis, which may recover over several weeks if the failure is not pro-longed. In prolonged insults to the kidney- acute cortical necrosis may occur and recovery from this is not so good. Good. Now tell me about renal failure as a result of renal causes?"

"Renal causes are those affecting the kidney itself- as in glomerulonephritis."

"Of which the cardinal features are?"

"Firstly Proteinuria, secondly Haematuria and thirdly, Urinary casts."

"Good. Good. Other renal causes include vasculitis, nephrotoxic drugs, rhabdomyolysis, interstitial nephritis, haemolytic/uraemic syndrome and myeloma. Got that?" Merlin removed the infusion of Hartmann's which was running into Viktor's arm. What was he going to do?

"Yes got that. Doctor Merlin- should we not start giving the fluids and antibiotics now?" Ian asked impatiently. The hairs on the back of his neck stood on end, and a cold sweat ran down his back.

"All in good time boy." Merlin replied. "And before I get into that- tell me the post-renal causes of renal failure."

Ian searched his brain and entered the kidney room, which in the white city was depicted as something similar to the chocolate river in Willy Wonker's chocolate factory. "Well these include anything in the urinary tract which might alter the function of the kidneys. Obstruction is the primary modality which induces the kidneys to fail and this can occur at any sight within the urinary tract. Common causes are prostatic hypertrophy, carcinoma of the prostate, ureteric stones, tumours of the renal pelvis, ureters or bladder including those externally compressing these structures- oh and retroperitoneal fibrosis."

"Good. Also bear in mind that advanced renal failure will only occur with the obstruction of both kidneys." Merlin took out what looked like the equipment to perform an arterial blood gas. "Now, with arterial blood gases, feel for the radial pulse- feel where it is strongest- make sure you have squeezed the syringe of heparin, hold the needle like a pen and go for it." He demonstrated to Ian- why was he showing him how to perform an arterial blood gas? "We used to do this by venous circulation, but that takes an awful amount of time. This way is much quicker." Merlin stabbed into his arm, and almost immediately blood began to pump into the syringe. He went to a blood gas reader at the side of the room and squirted it inside. He read the print out and screwed up the paper. Right, good, that's enough now I think.

As the blood ran out of the man's arm, colour had drained from his face- and Ian wondered if he should have stopped this from happening earlier? But who was he to challenge Doctor Merlin? He was a mere medical student! And he had signed up for this- the man was a killer- he deserved it! But then did anyone deserve this? Even for the most heinous of crimes? Was that not why they lived in a democracy? The bucket filled more and more, and the patient looked paler and paler. Ian willed Merlin to work quicker. Before Ian had had time to speak again, the bucket was full and Merlin had pulled out the arterial drip. Ian felt sick. It was if they had dropped to this criminal's level. But it was done?

"So if you now check his pulse, he will be tachycardic?" Ian felt his pulse- it was racing and at approximately 120 per minute. "And measure his blood pressure- this will be low? He will be starting to elicit signs of shock."

"How do we stop this?" Ian asked.

"Well that is what I ask you my boy?" Merlin stood still, staring.

"ABCDE's?" Ian blurted out immediately.

"Yes, true, but that is a given boy- you cannot simply blurt out ABCDE's for everything I ask you, tell me how ultimately you will fix this?"

"Well, he is dehydrated and septic so I'd like to re-perfuse him? As well as giving him some crucial antibiotics."

"Yes good- what fluid will you give?"

"An infusion of colloid? Gelofusine or something similar?"

"Why a colloid infusion and not a crystalloid one?"

"It is suggested that colloids stay in the intravascular space longer than crystalloids?"

"True- though not sure how much proof there is for this. In truth, get as much fluid into him as you can- within the limits of over perfusing him and causing him to go into fluid overload and pulmonary oedema- do this by crucially assessing fluid status. Roughly, what has come out should go in. Urinary catheters are very useful for measuring this, but sometimes nursing notes of urine output will do just as good a job."

"Ok." Ian said grabbing a litre bag of Hartmann's. He attached it to the drip line and cannula, and began to squeeze it into the man. Merlin saw this and grinned.

"If we did not know what the cause of the renal failure was, we would want an urgent renal ultrasound to look for any obstruction which will manifest as urinary tract dilatation, particularly hydronephrosis."

Ian did not really hear what Merlin had said, he urgently tried to squeeze the bag of Hartmann's into Viktor. When it had run out, he began to draw another bag of Hartmann's solution up and attach it to the infusion. Merlin again grinned.

"Perhaps is now also a good time to discuss fluid balance and maintenance?"

Ian thought it was in fact a terrible time to discuss it, but who was he to argue? He had to do what Merlin said in order to be accepted into this organisation. This organisation which he so wanted to be a part of. "What are the normal daily requirements of fluids- as in how much water do we need per day?"

"Approximately 4 litres, slightly less for women and more for men."

"Correct."

"And how much urine should we produce in a normal day?"

"1 or 2 litres?"

"Yes, between that."

"And how much fluid do we have going around our body on average?"

"Well, approximately 6 litres intra-vascularly- 1 litre in third space losses- breathing and so on."

"Okay. Good. Largely with fluid maintenance, we try to put in what goes out- so measuring urinary output is key- often kindly checked by nurses for us."

"Okay."

"What components does 0.9% Normal Saline have in it?"

"0.9% % sodium chloride?" Ian thought that was obvious.

"Good. And Hartmann's solution?"

"Sodium, Chloride, lactate and a small amount of potassium."

"Good. Is sometimes called 'Ringers Lactate.' And what is a complication of renal failure commonly leading to death?"

Ian suddenly stopped the Hartmann's. Hyperkalaemia was common with acute renal failure, and here he was pumping litre after litre of a fluid containing potassium into Viktor. "This is why we monitor his ECG- hyperkalaemia is life threatening which can produce cardiac arrhythmias such as ventricular defibrillation and asystole. ECG changes with hyperkalaemia include peaked T waves, a widened QRS complex, absent P waves and a sine wave appearance. After measuring potassium levels urgently or if ECG changes are present, one must treat with Calcium, insulin and glucose as well as oral or rectal Calcium Resonium. Urgent dialysis treatment should also be arranged. Other serious complications of acute renal failure include metabolic acidosis, encephalopathy and pericarditis. But to be honest, we do not have any of these treatments available. So Viktor is going to have to manage without them, and we will see how he does. If he dies- well he has had it coming." Merlin said this very coldly, staring at him as if he had personally been hurt by him. It made Ian wonder about Merlin's past. He seemed to be out of the room for a moment. Ian thought that as he gazed into nothingness- he aged perhaps twenty years. Merlin snapped out of it, and appeared his normal self again.

"Good. Luckily for you, Hartmanns has a very minimal amount of potassium in it compared to other components. Nevertheless perhaps give him some normal saline, I'll bring him out of the general anaesthetic. Well done Ian."

Knackered- Ian made his way out of the priory. Thoughts of Viktor Franzech, of Acute Renal Failure and of where on earth Dr Merlin had been trained filled his brain. But they would have to be removed- he had a date! He pulled out his mobile phone, took a deep breath as butterflies filled his chest and dialled Kate, the waitress's number.

They met at the pub down the road half an hour later. What a distraction to take Ian's mind off Merlin. As Kate and he flirted, what Ian did not know what that it would not be until his finals exam when he would find out about Merlin's background and he had no idea how much he did not know. But for the time being, Ian did not care as he asked if she wanted to come back to his for coffee.

Chapter Eleven: The Burning Man

The next day, hungover but fairly satisfied with how his night had gone (he had walked Kate to the metro station earlier that morning,) he faced Merlin in the cold stone room as he stood in front of the noteboard. Merlin invited someone else into the room, and Ian recognised him as the man who had greeted him at the very beginning of all of this at Tynemouth. Merlin offered him a seat.

"Ian you have met Alf before I believe?"

"Yes, briefly!" He smiled. Alf, the man who had first escorted Ian into the priory, did not smile back.

"Good. Alf has kindly agreed to come and help with your teaching today. He has a problem which I would like you to think about." Oh what was it now, Ian sighed to himself waiting for the emergency, the insulin syringe, the poisoned mug of tea. But none of this came. The man was clearly edgy- fidgeting in his seat. What, he wondered, might be wrong with him?

He glanced at one of the lanterns on the wall. In the background he heard the dripping of water echoing about the dungeon. "Perhaps you'd like to tell me what your problems are Alf?"

"I'm sure Alf has many problems, just ask about medical problems or we'll be here all day." Dr Merlin interrupted, winking at Alf. Alf looked at him but did not smile.

"Sorry."

Alf started without further prompting. "I have been having nightmares..." He paused and looked uneasily at Dr Merlin. Dr Merlin smiled back. It was strange, behind the firm and clinical eyes which so often found Ian, he saw something different. A kindness. A trust.

"I... I'm sorry its just I find it difficult to talk about it."

"That's ok- take as long as you like." Ian smiled at him, although again the smile was not returned.

"I keep having the same nightmare...and it haunts me during the day as well... it's like I just can't get it out of my life... I don't know what it is- but it scares me to my very soul... I think it could be the devil talking to me."

Ian felt baffled. Nightmares? Where was this in the textbooks? "Go on Alf? Perhaps tell me what happens?"

Alf again glanced at Dr Merlin who nodded understandingly. "We can stop whenever you like. Please take your time Alf, I know it's hard." Alf nodded at Dr

Merlin and stared at the floor. After a few minutes of silence, he continued.

"Well... For some time now, I have been having nightmares... I..." He looked quite pale, as if a shiver had shot down his spine. He stared directly into Ian's eyes.

"I go to sleep, and as soon as I do, I am greeted by a man who is on fire. Everything around is just blackness except the man. He is laughing- laughing at me. I can smell the burning- I can smell his flesh burning. He comes over to me and whispers to me- all sorts of things- nasty things... And then..." He had begun to shake. "And then- he sets light to me." This last sentence he said very coldly, as if he was struggling still to understand. "I then, wake up in a cold sweat, sometimes screaming. And I am scared to go to sleep now, I just cant sleep."

"May I ask did this follow a traumatic event in your life?" Merlin raised his eyebrows at the question. Ian knew PTSD or post traumatic stress disorder caused intense and vivid nightmares.

"Ok that is enough for now." Merlin said. That is great, Ill come to see you in ten minutes upstairs Alf. Thank you." He ushered him out of the room, Ian thought rather prematurely in his opinion.

"Thank you!" Ian said to Alf, but he was already shuffling out of the room. Merlin disappeared for a few minutes and then returned.

"Right what is causing this boy?"

"Schizophrenia?" Ian came out with, it was all he could think of from what he had gathered. Dr Merlin sighed.

"Schizophrenia. Hmmm... Not the worst diagnosis in the world, but incorrect. No evidence of auditory hallucinations- Remember mental illness must fit the ICD-10 criteria. No, nightmares- nightmares boy! Come on use your head now."

"Depression with psychosis?" Dr Merlin stood up and paced.

"You label him with a mental health problem after I have just said think of the ICD-10 criteria? You have fallen into the trap of ruling out organic disease before looking to psychiatry! Think boy! What might cause nightmares boy? Specifically nightmares?"

"Dementia?" Ian had had hardly any time to think about it, so why would he be able to tell without guessing? He had no crystal ball!

"If you are not going to think through logically, then I will tell you for you have clearly not done your reading!" He gave Ian a piercing look which made him sit upright.

"I'll give you a clue… Alfred covers up his symptoms very well…" Ian felt baffled. What symptoms?

"Symptoms of what?" He asked.

"Tell me how he was sitting. He was sitting comfortably?"

Ian thought back. He remembered the fidgeting. And the blank face.

"Well no he kept sort of fidgeting?"

"Fidgeting? Or moving involuntarily?"

"Well- I did not look closely enough?"

"Well if you had you would have guessed- if I say the words shuffling gait and resting tremor would they mean anything to you?" Then it clicked, Ian thought of it straight away after such a big clue.

"He has Parkinson's Disease!"

"Good! Go on boy."

"Well, he gave the impression of being depressed as he spoke with quite a monotonous voice- and he fidgeted a lot- but actually he was covering his tremor- of course- and yes he was slower than perhaps he should have been when he moved- Bradykinesia? The monotonous voice is a result of him having Parkinson's! And his blank face is because his face cannot display expressions!"

"Finally." Dr Merlin seemed pleased, even if it had taken a while to figure it out. "Alfred's Parkinson's is very, very subtle. He is embarrassed about it and covers it very well. Poor man." He paused for a moment. "So what is causing his nightmares boy?"

"His medication?"

"Good how? And which one? In fact start by running through everything you know about Parkinson's." Ian's heart sank. He knew bits, but not all.

"Well... It is characterized by as I said earlier, Bradykinesia or slowness of movement, a resting tremor of 4-6hz I believe- and rigidity..."

"What causes it?"

"I'm not sure..."

"Good as neither are many people. There are theories of course." Ian felt relieved as Merlin began one of his rambles where he enjoyed listening to the sound of his own voice. This would give him a break from questioning for a while. Dr Merlin talked for a few minutes about a toxin called MPTP or 1-methyl-4-phenyl-1,2,3,6-tetrahydropyridine which caused degeneration of a tract in the brain. Ian switched off as soon as Merlin said MPTP in full however and didn't hear much of it.

"Good. So remind me of the pathology in the brain now boy?"

Ian thought about what he knew and tried to answer without making it obvious he had not listened. "Parkinson's arises due to degradation in the Dopaminergic NigroStriatal tract… which is situated in the Substantia Nigra I think."

"Correct- go on."

"Well- I believe Lewy Bodies present in this area are suggestive of Parkinson's."

"Good- now talk about the three main characteristics a bit more please- it is not enough to say tremor, rigidity and Bradykinesia. As Alfred displayed, patients can be subtle- what might we look for?"

"The tremor is most marked when the patient is at rest, and it is usually a rolling of thumb over fingers?" Ian wondered how Alfred covered this up, for he did not notice it at all, bar the fidgeting.

"And rigidity?"

"Well...Rigidity is equal across both flexors and extensor muscles...unlike in spasticity that is." He quickly clarified himself. "And in Bradykinesia they can have a shuffling walk or gait... and they freeze- as in find it difficult to go through a door without stopping...and again, monotonous voice and an expressionless face..."

"Right that's enough. So what medication is causing his nightmares?" Ian had no clue.

"Ever heard of Entacapone?"

"I have?"

"There are some links to various medications for Parkinsons and nightmares- entacapone being one of them. Good. That is enough of that, we will not go into this in much more detail- it is hardly emergency training. Ok. You have now completed several stages in your training before your deployment. You are now ready to go onto pre-deployment training on the helicopters. You will join the emergency response teams in the UK and Ill talk you through what to do with patients on the radioset, just as will be the case in Iraq. Excellent. Come with me and we will get you your kit issued, and go through how the headsets work as well as how to repair them. This form of communications will not only be your lifeline to me, but also the patients who you are treating. Well done Ian, not long left now before you will be tested to your limits. Well done." Merlin led out of the room, and so began Ian's pre-deployment training.

Chapter Eleven: Helicopter Training

One week later, despite a lot of military training, Ian was bored of waiting. He had been waiting for what seemed to be ages now. He just wanted to get on with it. The military firing ranges at Catterick Garrison would have been quite fun, if it were not for the reality of Ian's actually having to fire a rifle or pistol, or throw a grenade. He was not sure if he would fancy that. At least he was carrying a pistol and a rifle, and would be under much protection. They could do some damage if he needed them. But what if he came into a position where he was not under protection? He thought again about the thought of going to Iraq, and it made him incredibly nervous. But he had to do it? That was where his final test was- his exam to pass out into the secret doctors! And how much he wanted to do it, how much he needed to!

Sipping his mug of tea, he looked out of the window as the rain pitter-pattered onto it, and eyed over the yellow sea king helicopter which was to be his ambulance for the next however long- "until you have dealt with more acute things. Get your adrenaline pumping and so on in an evacuation scenario." Merlin had said. Bloody Merlin. What did he know? Quite a lot actually, Ian thought to himself. He waited longer and longer, until the third cup of tea became the eighth, and the eighth became the thirteenth. And then, the red telephone rang. Ian answered it anxiously, his heart skipping a beat.

"MERT here, Ian Mellows medical student speaking."

"Hello, we have a man with chest pain in his house in the cheviots hills. It will be too long before an ambulance can reach him. Suspected acute cardiac event. Coordinates have been radioed through to the pilot. Make sure you take your other radio to get hold of Merlin. Out."

Ian grabbed the small neat radio set which had been given to him by Merlin. Apparently, it was something he could call for help on- a specialist satellite phone which was no larger than a mobile. Apparently, so he was told- it would work in any part of the world, no matter where. The new technology within it was highly secret, but using a series of wavelengths and frequencies and other weird and wonderful physics, Ian had a link with whoever had one of the other halves to this radio set. It was a small comfort, if anything. He would much rather have actually had Merlin there in person!

He grabbed his helmet, and ran out to the chopper. The crew were already aboard. He had not really spoken to them, but they seemed friendly enough. He climbed on board and fastened himself in. The chopper started up. It grew to a deafening roar. The crew member next to him mouthed something to him. He had no chance of hearing him. He mouthed again, and then leant over to Ian and switched on his headphones for he had them on mute. Ian went red. The man smiled from behind his moustache. "I said he is a diabetic! Likely MI. I know you are supposed to do this by yourself matey, but I'm about if you want some help."

"Cheers." Ian smiled nervously, hiding his real feelings of absolute panic. Bloody Merlin! The helicopter had lifted off now, and they were flying over Newcastle.

"Flight time ten minutes." He heard the pilot mutter.

"You just ask me for what you need ok Ian, I'll hand it to you- don't worry that you don't know what it's all called yet." He winked. Ian thanked god this guy was about. What was his name? He racked his brains. He did not even know the paramedic's name! What a mess he was in! Too late to ask him now he thought.

They continued to fly, now heading over rolling green hills which would have been beautiful to Ian had he not been about to have an MI himself from the worry. "There is the valley." Came over the radio, the pilot suggesting they put down in the field next to the farmhouse. Ian could see a group of people waving at them, small dots in the distance now getting bigger by the second. And to think they were to rely on him! His heart beat even harder now, and sweat poured off him.

They touched down, and the other slightly smaller man near the man with the moustache pulled open the slide door. Ian tried to get out, but had left his seat belt buckles done up. Feeling stupid, he un did them and rushed over to the nearest person he could find shaking their hand. "Thank you for coming doctor, he is in a bad way- a lot of pain. He is in the top room."

"Ok thank you, would you take me to him please."

"Of course." The woman's eyes were red, and he guessed her to be a neighbour. They rushed through the front gate and into the house. Ian thought for a moment he should take his shoes off it was so tidy, but over rode this thought with panic and carried on upstairs. A man was sitting on the floor against the edge of the bed. He had brown hair, was wearing a dark blue polo shirt and was incredibly breathless. Ian made his initial assessment.

"Hello sir-" But the man stopped himself talking as it was too much pain. He was breathing. He could not hear any stridor particularly, so he seemed to have an airway. His breathing was fast. A respiratory rate of 25 Ian counted. He was red in the face, he took his pulse. It was weak and thready. "Tell me where it hurts?" Ian said to the man. The man simply pointed at his chest and made a fist. "I'd like to give him some morphine please." He said to the paramedic. "What route and how much sir?" He asked quickly, reaching down into his bag.

"IV. Please… Dose… Err." He took out his BNF. He looked up morphine. "Errr…"

"It's a dose of 5-10mg, as well as an antiemetic such as metoclopramide 10mg." The paramedic said, winking. Ian showed his appreciation by nodding, but was too preoccupied to go into an overwhelming thank you.

"Could we get some oxygen on him please."

"How much?"

"15 litres at 100%"

"Yes."

"And some nitrates."

"Which ones?"

"Err…Just nitrates."

"Which ones?"

"Any! Just give him any!" The paramedic thought better of pushing this and pulled out some Glyceryl Trinitrate.

"He needs some aspirin, and some clopidogrel now too."

"Dose?" Paramedic asked, drawing up the nitrites. Ian got out his BNF again.

"Each 300 mg."

"Ok. And then what?"

"Lets get him into hospital so we can measure his Troponin I and T, Creatine Kinase and do an ECG. Then we can go from there."

The other chopper hand brought up a stretcher, and they started to carefully sit him into it (it had a chair component to it). They then carried him out carefully out of the house, and down the stairs- out of his front door and into the chopper.

The pilot had not stopped the engine, and they slowly took off, waving too his family and few neighbours that were around him in the small valley. They headed back to not the Royal Victoria Infirmary, but the priory at Tynemouth, where Dr Merlin awaited.

The chopper touched down on the grass outside the priory. Merlin was standing waiting, walking stick in hand and looking stern. How he irritated Ian sometimes with his smugness. He could not help but respect him though. He had ordered the paramedics to take the man into the ward, and run perform the tests Ian had asked for.

"So Mellows. Differential diagnosis?"

Ian racked his brains.

"I think it is fairly clear he has an acute coronary syndrome. But I would wish to wait and see the investigations to confirm it."

"Good. So you have not seen them. Differentials for chest pain? Talk me through system by system, always a good point to start."

"Well, I suppose in terms of respiratory, he might have a pneumothorax or pleuritic pain? Or even a carcinoma? Or even Pulmonary embolus."

"Good Cardio?"

"Many, but Myocardial Infarct top of the list."

"Neuro?"

"Err... Not many I can think of."

"No there are not. Musculo-skeletal?"

"Well Chest wall pain? Costo-chondritis?"

"Good, Gastro-intestinal system?"

"Well- perhaps Gastro Oesophageal Reflux disease? Or Peptic ulcer?"

"Good good stop there. So I am as you have said rather certain he is having an acute cardiac event, simply from the history. Tell me what causes these Mellows?"

"Well... A blocked coronary artery causing lack of blood supply to an area of the heart?" He looked at Merlin hopeful.

"Yes- MI occurs when cardiac monocytes die due to this lack of blood and therefore oxygen supply. The most common mechanism to all acute coronary syndromes is rupture of a cap of a plaque within a coronary artery." They had now reached the door to the passageway which led towards the ward. The paramedics had disappeared deep within the priory now, and were hopefully organising all of the tests. Merlin waved Ian through the door, and then continued. "As a result of the ruptured plaque, platelets clump together in the coronary arteries, you get thrombosis and vasoconstriction. As the platelets aggregate, they release serotonin and thromboxane A2- which causes this thrombus to form and the vasoconstriction associated- which lastly results in the myocardial ischemia and death of monocytes due to a reduction in coronary blood flow. Understand?"

"Err..."

"Yes its complicated, but it will come. Most important thing is that you administered Morphine, Oxygen, Nitrates, Aspirin and Clopidegrel as fast as possible. Remember, cardiac monocyte death is irreversible, unlike many other tissues."

Ian felt himself grow slightly, it was rare for Merlin to give him a compliment, and even though this seemed to be an indirect one, it was a compliment nonetheless Ian thought. They arrived at the door to the ward, and entered. The patient was laying on one of the beds, ECG leads dotted all over him. Merlin printed off an ECG and handed it to Ian. "Interpret this please. And which tests did you send for again Mellows?"

"Troponin I and T, Creatine Kinase MB, Full blood count, serum electrolytes, glucose and lipid profile."

"Good, when do Troponins peak?"

"After 12 hours."

"Good- and why a full blood count?"

"Perhaps anaemia could be a cause?"

"Good- ECG?"

Ian looked it over. It was the correct patient's, it was a 10 second strip at 25mm/second. There were regular PQRS complexes, and the rate was 66 beats per minute. He could see ECG changes in the leads which faced the area of the heart concerned. "Anterior myocardial infarction- there is ST elevation in leads V1 to V3."

"Good. What leads would you see and inferior infarct in?"

"leads II, III and AVF."

"Lateral?"

"Lead I, AVL and V5 or V6."

"And with posterior?" He smiled now, Ian thought he knew he would catch him out at some point. But he would not let him.

"Posterior MI shows ST depression in leads V1-V3 with a dominant R wave, and ST elevation in V5 or V6."

"Good Mellows. Very good." He paced across to the window. "Very good indeed." He walked over to the patient. "You have had some trouble with your heart my friend, I will explain it to you when you are feeling a bit less tired okay?" The man nodded, and lay his head down. He looked better than he had done, but still very ill. "Come with me." Merlin gestured to Ian. He followed, and they walked up the steps to the room where he had first met Merlin. Merlin got out his pipe, lit it and began to smoke. He took some brandy from the cabinet, got two of the crystal glasses and poured some into it.

"Good Mellows. Very good." He puffed away for some time, and they both sat quite still and quiet. Ian enjoyed the rest. How odd for Merlin of all people to be saying 'very good' all the time."

Eventually, he began to speak again. "Good. You are ready to go now Ian."

"To go where?" Ian asked naively. Merlin smiled, and shook his head briefly. He took out his mobile phone and pressed a speed dial number. Someone answered on the other end.

"Klaus Merlin here. He is ready to leave. Send the transport as soon as you can. Uh huh- half an hour? Good. Very good. Thanks." He put the phone on the table.

"You are ready to go to Iraq, and sit your final assessment."

Even though he had been expecting it, it hit Ian hard. His breathing increased, and his palms became incredibly sweaty. He felt the blood run into his cheeks. Nervousness and fear gripped him.

"Now?" He asked.

"Yes now. This is how it works Ian, remember the secrecy documents you signed. Remember the contract. Your final exam is conducted in *circumstances a normal doctor would not face.* And do not forget it. You will have some in the field training, and when it is time- your exam will be upon you. Do not fret my boy, from the way you just handled that case- I can see you are ready."

"But I don't feel ready?" Ian wanted to run, run away as fast as he could. But he knew that this was what he signed up for, and finally the time to prove himself was here.

"Can I call my family?"

"You can call them- but remember, you must tell them nothing of this- you have been selected to go on a medical intensive care course, and you will not be back for a few days. We can keep them updated as things happen."

"But what if something happens to me?" Merlin paused and walked over to the window. Staring at the sea he answered.

"Yes there is a chance of this- there is. On the plane we will ask you to write your will. But do not fret my boy- do not fret. This experience will make you a man, and a fully pledged member of the secret service doctors. And for this privilege, many people would die, you mark my words." Ian sat up sternly in his chair. Anxious as ever, he waited for what seemed like an age as the minutes counted down to the helicopter coming in to pick him up. And when he heard the blades go around and around, he grabbed his bag of kit and swung it onto his back. Anxious but also excited, he did not know what was ahead. Both of them, Merlin and Ian walked up to the neatly kempt grass and the ruined chapel on the hill as the helicopter blades of a Chinook thundered around and around. And he shook Merlin's hand, and with a look of good luck and a reminder to use his radio set to get him when he needed him- he walked up the entrance ramp to the Chinook and was greeted by a well built gunner who had dark sunglasses on. "Flight time is about 30 minutes to Brize Norton, and then you'll transfer to a plane. You will then have a flight time of 5 hours to Jordan, where you will transfer back to a Chinook. Your next stop after that will be within Iraq."

"Where in Iraq?"

"That's secret presently sir. Just sit back and enjoy the flight."

Chapter Twelve: Iraq

All the flights ran smoothly, but this did not take away from the anxious feeling in Ian's stomach. He had just had to write a will, and that had been far from easy. How does one write a will to those you love, without tempting fate? He had made a very quick note saying it could all go to his mum, and then, after getting the pilot to witness it, sat back down and tried to sleep. His poor mum did not even know where he was! Probably for the best, she was a worrier, Ian thought. He had been dropped at the main British base, and transferred onto another helicopter after getting kitted out with some extra desert fighting equipment. He was also issued his own morphine and pistol ammunition. He was asked if he wanted a rifle, and thinking it probably was a good idea, went for a shotgun, rather than an assault rifle. That would do some damage if he needed it, he thought and it gave him confidence. Ian sat on the Chinook, and was now flying into a forward operating base in Iraq, just outside Baghdad. He had learnt to ignore most of the calls over his earphones on this helicopter, until he heard: "We're re-routing. We've had a call from a patrol medic requesting a doctor."

Ian leant over to the gunner. "I'm not a doctor." He pleaded.

"You're as good as one. If you don't like it, I'm afraid it's tough- there's no-one else for miles."

"Re-routing where to anyway?"

"Just a small village slightly off the route, we won't be long."

"You sure no-one else can go?"

"Yes very sure. Look it won't take long."

The gunner pushed his visor back down over his eyes and the Chinook lurched heavily to one side. Land filled the small, round windows and he could see many Arabic houses in the distance as well as a small mosque. The sound of metal pinging sharply against metal rattled at the bottom of the helicopter and the gunner on the rear of the helicopter swung his machine gun round to aim at something on the ground. He did not, however, fire at anything. Ian heard through the radio, "small pocket of militants amongst some Bedouin huts. Call it in- they shouldn't be a bother to us." The pilot continued unworried. Ian however, felt so worried he thought he might urinate.

He fought his nerves all he could. He had to appear calm, even though inside he was torn apart by anxiety and fear. What were they being re-routed for? What needed a doctor that a patrol medic could not handle? He checked once again the radio set Merlin had given him. He gave a radio-check signal, and sure enough over the sound of the helicopter he could just make out Merlin's voice back in the UK, probably annoying someone. But now Ian was glad of it. He knew he could ask him anything, and, in his experience, Merlin would know the answer. Even if he did give this answer in a very annoying manner.

The helicopter glided to a static hover in the air and gradually sunk lower and lower until a soft bump saw them land. "We'll stay here. If it gets hot- we won't wait around. Get back as soon as- or we won't be here to give you a lift." The gunner smiled and tapped Ian on his helmet. "Got your gas mask?" He asked. "Yes. Why?" Saddam Hussein used chemical weapons before, which means they are out there. It's worth making sure you have it on you. He winked. Ian gulped. Before he could argue, he was bundled out of the helicopter and was shaking hands with a man head to toe in body armour. His arm bore both a red cross and a red crescent symbol on a white armband. Heat belted Ian in the face, and he was drenched in sweat already. The man had his rifle slung, and his face was coated in dust.

"Paediatric case!" The sergeant bellowed over the sound of the rotary blades. Ian held his hands tightly to his face as sand and dust were hurled into him. He nodded. "Young lad. Can't make out what's wrong with him- I've only done the combat med tech's course- my expertise don't stretch to civvies' stuff!" They were far away enough from the chopper now for Ian to lower his arms.

"Okay, where is he?"

"This way sir."

The medic led him through a gap in some houses. The heat was immense. Ian was so nervous about the casualty that he forgot to even notice this was the first time he had set foot in an Arabic land outside the wire- he was in a war zone! He slung his shotgun over his back and opened his desert parka jacket. His med kit swung against his leg, but he left his body armour firmly where it is.

They walked briskly down some very tight, dusty alleyways and came onto an open tiled yard between several houses. A woman wrapped in black shawls came running to him and pleaded with him in Arabic. "His mother I think- can't make out a word."

"Is there an interpreter?"

"No- can't get one."

"Not even on the radio?"

"They're trying but apparently there's a mass casualty gone into Basra hospital and they're all in use." He smiled. "I'm sure we'll make do."

Ian was however, not so sure. He was shown into a very dark room by the still panicked mother, and onto a low bed where lay a boy of perhaps 12. "Hello mate." Ian said kneeling down to look at the boy. The boy did not respond. In the dim light, Ian could see he was very ill. He was crying silently. The woman was making all sorts of gestures and bizarre actions which Ian could not guess for one moment the meaning to.

She would put her hand to her head, start shaking like a mad chicken, then touch her neck, then pick at her arm, then shake and then point at the boy. She would then repeat the process, as if she had rehearsed it. "She's been doing that since we got here. I can't for the life of me make it out."

"Neither can I." Ian retorted. He took out the radio set, his direct link to Merlin, and called him on it. "Where do I even start?!" He asked confused.

"Find someone who can speak Arabic in the correct dialect."

"There is no-one." Ian replied.

"No-one?"

"No-one." Ian replied stumped.

"Fine. Put me on loudspeaker so the mother can hear."

"Okay..." Ian said, confused. He moved the radio over towards the dancing mother. Surely Merlin did not speak Arabic?!

"Al-Salamo alay-kum, ana min Tynemouth fee Engletera, ana Tabib..." Ian shook his head in disbelief. What next should he expect from that man?

The woman listened intently. She then started to speak into the radio in response. Ian and the medic stood in a bemused, yet impressed silence. Merlin spoke in English suddenly, and the mother gazed at Ian wide eyed.

"I can't speak her exact dialect Mellows, but can get close enough to get the gist- look at his skin. Apparently he has a rash. Check it for me would you?"

Ian took a small tea glass which was on the room's low table and rolled it over a rash he found on the boys abdomen. It did not disappear when he pressed on it.

"It's non-blanching." He said into the radio which the patrol medic was now holding.

"Right. His mother suggests he has neck pains, headache and photophobia, hence why I expect, you are in a very dark room. Correct?"

"Correct."

"I want you to examine for Kernig's sign."

"What is that?"

"Pain and resistance on passive knee extension with the hip fully flexed."

Low and behold, the child made a blood curdling scream when Ian did the examination. "He has been having seizures as well. I suspect this is Meningitis. We must not delay. Get an IV infusion in and give him fluids and Benzylpenicillin. The common organisms are Meningococcus, Pneumococcus, Haemophilus Influenzae and Listeria Monocytogenes. We could do with getting some oxygen and fluids as well. Ideally we want to investigate him. Perform U and E's, FBC, LFT, glucose and a coagulation screen."

"Right." Ian jotted some notes on his rubber glove.

"Also, do a full septic screen. A blood culture, throat swabs, one for bacteria one for viruses and a stool sample for viruses. Need to be careful with regards lumbar puncture. He has been having seizures so it may be best to avoid for the time being. If he had access to a CT scan and CXR that would be ideal but I suppose this is unlikely. We could perhaps give some cefotaxime as well, until we are sure of the causative organism. Can we get him the right meds if we identify the organism, or is this all a waste of time?" Merlin asked sceptically.

Ian looked at the medic as the distant hum of the helicopter rotary blades vibrated through the room. He nodded. "We'll be around here for a while. If you tell us what to give him and give us it- we'll see he gets it alright."

"Yes we can." Ian confirmed into the receiver.

"Good. Now let me speak to the mother again."

After some more conversation between Merlin and the mother on the radio, and after Ian had done all Merlin had said, taking bloods and putting them into a portable storage container, the woman hugged both him and the medic, tears streaming from her eyes. Ian bade her farewell and walked out of the door to make his way back to the chopper.

Chapter Thirteen: Ambush

"One more patient we need you to see if you don't mind sir." Ian's heart sank.

"What?" He ejected. The combat medical technician continued un-phased.

"Woman with cancer- could do with some pain relief. It's a terminal diagnosis.

"Do we actually have time?" He looked at his watch agitatedly, not knowing what time they even left the chinook.

"Should do, won't be long. She's in a lot of pain."

"Oh alright, just make it quick for goodness sake." Ian was again led down a series of streets and archways and around low hanging ceilings and dark passageways, until he was met by a man of around his own age. He spoke near perfect English.

"I am Maljef, a police medic here. I have been tending to this woman for some time, but we know that she does not have long. This is what the previous doctor noted." He handed Ian a scrawled on bit of scrunched up paper which read in scruffy handwriting: *Lung carcinoma, prognosis; one month.*

"When did he see her?" Ian asked.

"It was a woman. Perhaps two weeks ago. The medication she gave her has run out, and she is in much pain."

"Right please take me to her. What was she on?"

"Doesn't say, sorry." Ian rolled his eyes. He was led inside a low hanging door with a smell of a incense and Islamic prayers being played on a cassette player in the background. A lady of around fifty lay on the low bed, looking incredibly weak and frail. She did not smile at Ian.

"Anyone any idea what she has been on?" Ian asked looking around from person to person.

"Don't think anyone knows sir, sorry."

"Ok, one moment please." Ian took out the radioset and called for Merlin.

"Yes?"

"Woman with terminal carcinoma of the lung. Requires pain relief. Shall I go up the step up pain relief ladder?"

"First find out where the pain is boy- remember SOCRATES- Sight, onset, character, radiation, timing, exacerbating or alleviating factors and severity on a scale of one to ten. This allows us to work out the best type of medication to give her, as some work better for differing types of pain remember?"

"Yes, yes I will do and will get back to you." He walked over to the lady and tried to engage with her in English, but she merely shook her head.

"She only speaks Arabic. I will translate." Maljef looked poised and ready, clearly fond of the lady. Ian assessed all of SOCRATES. She had some pain in her upper back which was there all the time, and was sharp. It radiated to her neck. She also had pain in her right arm which was shooting. She had a headache too, which was there all the time and woke her up during the night. He relayed this to Merlin over the radio set.

"This is bad. I fear she may have spinal metastases and possible brain metastases too. Any headache that wakes you during the night suggests increased intra-cranial pressure. And the pain in the back. Does she have any incontinence, lack of motor or sensory function in the lower limbs?" Ian asked, and she did not. "Well this is something we can be thankful for at least. She'd probably need decompressive surgery if she had. Anyhow, pain- how do you understand pain Mellows?

"It is an unpleasant sensory experience."

"Good. Pain signals themselves, begin by a peripheral receptor (nociceptor or mechanoreceptor) being stimulated which transmits a signal to the spinal cord (usually via A delta fibres which are myelinated, and C fibres which are unmyelinated). Before another signal is sent to the higher centres of the brain, a reflex signal is sent immediately back to the peripheral motor component of the affected body part, in order to remove it from the stimulus. So in order to treat pain, we have many medications."

Ian stood half listening. "Doctor Merlin we must hurry as the Chinook is waiting."

"I will be quick- we use the step up analgesia ladder for treating pain. My guess is that this woman is in a fair bit, so we will give her some stronger ones. Anyhow." He paused and there was some static over the radio. Ian heard a distant explosion, and some machine gun fire. He looked across the room panicked. "Doctor Merlin, you must hurry! I can hear gunfire in the distance!"

"You are in Iraq, of course you can hear gunfire in the distance!" Ian shook himself, it was after all quite far away. But thoughts of the ricochet which hit the Chinook when they flew in had gripped his mind, and all he wanted to do was run out of the room.

"So, step up analgesia. You start with Non-steroidal anti-inflammatory drugs. These work by inhibiting the Cyclo-oxygenase (COX) pathways. In this group is also

Paracetamol: Thought to inhibit COX 3 pathway." Ian took some paracetamol out of his medical bag. "Next there is tramadol, a centrally acting analgesic. Works by synergistic action of two pharmacological actions. Are you getting this boy?"

"Yes…" Ian took tramadol out of his bag.

"Remember not to give all of these at once for goodness sakes!"

"I will…" He said sarcastically. "What is next?"

"Opiates. Now be careful with opiates. Physiological and psychological dependence can occur to opiates (particularly morphine), and sudden withdrawal can induce a withdrawal syndrome. They are used to treat poorly localized pain. (ie. Visceral.) Morphine has various ranges of CNS effects. These include euphoria, analgesia, sedation, respiratory depression, 3rd nerve nucleus stimulation, nausea and vomiting to name but a few. It is metabolized in the liver. Tolerance occurs if used for long periods and it causes constipation, biliary spasm and Sphincter of Oddi constriction. Can also cause histamine release. Make sure to administer some laxatives with morphine."

"Ok."

"There is also Diamorphine or basically heroin."

"Heroin?"

"Yes Heroin." He continued as if he had told Ian it was cheese. "It has a faster onset when given by injection and is more lipid soluble than morphine. You could use fentanyl, a transdermal patch which releases the drug over time. Phenazocine is very potent and is used for pain of intense severity... Perhaps your patient might benefit, let me think." He paused for a while. "Let us explore all the options first. There is pethidine which has a rapid onset of action, but with this a short duration. It's metabolized in the liver. Take note Ian, Pethidine ha a serious interaction with Mono amine oxidase inhibitors."

"What about codeine?" Ian asked.

"Codeine is a good option in some patients, but causes constipation. I think in this lady's case it won't touch her pain. She probably wants morphine. Remember that in case of opiod over dose, administer IV NALOXONE. But I am sure you will remember this from your lessons on overdoses."

Ian nodded his head to that. He then searched in his bag. Merlin continued. "There are also things such as anti-epileptics which can help with pain." Ian had found a chronic pain booklet, which he opened. He turned to the page for anti-epileptics. He was not sure if this was relevant to this woman. By now he had lost his train of thought, and had stopped listening to Merlin. He just caught the end of his sentence. "One can also look at anti-depressants such as Amitryptlline for pain and there are also atypical drugs such as Nefopam."

Ian explained to the police medic as he gave him some medications (he was not going to give him all of those Merlin had said, some oral morphine was probably the best thing to give to make her comfortable as he had said earlier). Merlin still nattered on the radio, but Ian ignored him. He had to get out of there, for they had been far too long. Before he had time to think to leave, the door burst open to everyone in the room's dismay.

The Chinook gunner was wide eyed, white as a sheet and sweating. Maljef the policeman made an outraged cry from behind his shemagh and pulled the blanket further over the woman. The gunner took no notice and grabbed Ian by the arm.

"The signals blokes have picked up an enemy radio transmission. There's reports of an expected suicide attack in this village. Target's a western doctor." They had been betrayed. Ian's heart might have burst out of his chest it beat so hard. "We've got to get out of here now." He grabbed Ian by his parka. Before being able to say goodbye, he was bundled out of the house and onto the street.

"Just keep moving!" The gunner shouted, looking terrified. Ian looked left and right, but did not see Maljef. He was too far away now to go back. Would he be okay? Fear gripped him. All he wanted to do was be away from this place.

The harsh Iraqi sun beat against his face and a smell of fresh flat bread and spices met his nostrils. His blood ran cold. He sprinted after the gunner back towards the Chinook. "Where is he?!" Ian screamed, drenched in a cold sweat.

"We don't know, just keep moving!" The gunner shouted, still looking forward. There was a burst of machine gun fire somewhere, not too far away. They ran faster now. The streets were empty and Ian could not quite work out where they were. But he did not care he just wanted to be out of there. The dust crunched underfoot and bits of rubble tumbled where their boots kicked them aside. The deep rumble of the Chinook helicopter blades met their ears. They were near. He shot a glance down an alleyway to his left and saw a toddler dressed in a purple dish dash and torn sandals. The boy sat quietly on a step throwing pebbles at other pebbles.

A lot then happened at once.

Ian's face hit the body armour of the gunner in front, hard, crunching his nose. The gunner had stopped dead in his tracks. Hitting the back of him sent them into a fall and they crashed onto the dusty ground. A dull, superficial pain bit his face. Ian's nose was bleeding and his eyes watered. A low pitched ringing filled his ears- dust rushed into his nostrils amongst the blood and he spat. The gunner screamed in a panic, "Get back! Turn around! The other way!" A sharp pain grabbed Ian's knees where he had grazed them. He looked at the palm of his throbbing hand, a stream of blood running from it. His head was a blur. He stared ahead of him, struggling to focus. And then he saw what had made the gunner stop.

Thirty metres away down the quiet, wide alleyway in front of him, a man dressed in muddy jeans and a thick brown leather jacket stood. Why such a thick leather jacket in this heat? His arms were spread out wide as if pinned to a crucifix and his palms were pointing upwards. His gaze was fixated on the sky. Ian could not work out what he was doing. But he then saw the blocks of white plastic explosives strapped to his chest, wires running all around them. One of the wires led to a button in his hand. And then the man lowered his head and looked at them. His deep brown eyes were empty with acceptance, his arms pinned out rigid- bearing the detonating button. Then he ran towards them.

They fumbled frantically on the ground to get up. Sprinting back the way they came, their legs moved so fast they struggled not to trip over. Bustling, bounding, bundling towards the alleyway they had just passed, they rushed to get behind cover- or get anywhere away from the man about to martyr himself.

Was this it? Was he about to die? The seconds were like hours. Ten metres away they sprinted, eight metres away, six metres away, four metres, two metres, "Allahu Akhbar!" And the hollow, sharp boom of the explosion met them and they became deaf, and with a wall of air and sand and rubble and flesh, in a slow motioned spin, they began to fly.

Chapter Fourteen: Coughing Death

A sharp pain bit into Ian's buttock. He strained to open his eyes. He could not tell if they were open, or if indeed they were closed. Was he blind? They hurt, they were full of sand. Or stones? Or grit? Or what was it? And gradually his vision became slightly clearer, though not really that clear. A cloud of dust was all around him, he was engulfed by it. A deadly silence filled the cloud, and was all that there to comfort him. And again he heard the sound of the helicopter blades thumping against the air. He heard someone coughing, choking, spluttering. It was an unpleasant sound. In a desperate and confused state, he grabbed for his gas mask and put it on. It made him breath slightly easier, despite the taste of rubber. He crawled towards the coughing, because surely at the source of it was a person. He put his hand on something warm and soft. He did not look at what it was. He carried on crawling. He put his hand to his face. Something sharp and metallic was sticking in his arm. He pulled at it, but it caused him to bite down hard in agony and he left whatever it was where it was. He stood up, and held his shotgun tightly, ready to shoot. Were there enemy soldiers out there? Slowly he walked through the intense dust cloud, and neared the coughing sound.

He came across the gunner. He was laying by the edge of a house amongst a pile of rubble. He was semi-conscious and panting for breath hard. His leg was mangled, two bone stumps popped out and his foot hung off at an angle. It was clearly an open tibular-fibular break. Bad risk of infection, and ultimately amputation. The man clutched his chest. Ian crawled over to him. "You ok?" He coughed. He could not speak. Ian threw down his shotgun and went about dressing the leg and administering morphine. The man clutched his chest harder, and grimaced. He could probably deal with that later. Ian quickly felt his pulse. He was tachycardic. What could he do? He got out a tourniquet and placed it on the thigh- the man wailed in agony. The leg looked horrific, burnt flesh and blood was everywhere. Despite the morphine and shot of antibiotics, he did not settle. Ian thought maybe he needed more painkillers. He was about to give some when the man started to deteriorate and became less responsive. Ian reached into the medical bag for his stethoscope. He also felt for his belt and pulled out the radio set- his lifeline to Dr Merlin. Oh how he needed him now! Half of it came out of the bag in his hand, the other half remained. He nevertheless tried to turn it on, to transmit to Merlin. To get some help. Any help! But the radio set did not respond. It sat in his hand broken and useless. He searched for the other radio, and tried to call in the Chinook- some help of some sort!

But the radio was nowhere to be found, no matter how much he searched. He began to feel around on the dusty floor amongst the dark dust cloud which still surrounded them, desperately he tried to find the radio- but he could not find it. And now the gunner was becoming more unresponsive- his breathing was becoming less strained. He then became unconscious. "ABCs you fuckwit!" Ian shouted at himself. He had done the classic thing of being distracted by the huge open fracture, and had not assessed the man's vital signs and checked for immediate life threatening injuries!

He checked his airway, it was clear. His breathing was now difficult, and he no longer coughed. He looked for bilateral chest expansion, but one side of the chest was hyperinflated and hyperresonant with absent breath sounds. Tension pneumothorax? He felt for tracheal deviation- knowing that if this was present, it was an incredibly late sign and he should have already acted if it was what he thought. All he could think of were the 4 H's and 4 T's of reversible causes of cardiac arrest. But were these applicable here? He tried to think of the military ones which Jim had taught him, but amongst his chokes and the darkness of the dust cloud- he could not remember. He thought of the books. He thought of the way his friend at medical school had told him to remember it. 'Imagine a depressed patient who tries to kill themselves. They take a load of medications, stab themselves in the chest, slit their wrists and jump into a lake. Therefore they get the reversible 4Hs and 4Ts of cardiac arrest- hypothermia, hypovolaemia, hypoxia, hyperkalaemia (metabolic) as well as toxins, tamponade, thrombus and tension pneumothorax.'

Ian shook himself and spoke aloud, running through the possibilities of what the gunner had. "Hypothermia- Unlikely, Hypoxia- maybe? Hyperkalaemia and metabolic- unlikely from trauma! Hypovolaemia- was he bleeding? He exposed him but could not determine any source of haemorrhage as the tourniquet had stopped the leg bleeding- unless it was internal? Tamponade- possible, tension pneumothorax- very possibly, thrombus- unlikely, toxins- well he had just given him a load of morphine- could that be it? At that dose?" He looked at the man hard, and noticed his neck veins were distended. Tension. It had to be a tension pneumothorax.

Ian had to act now or he would die. He pulled out a large bore cannula. He cut off the gunner's jacket, and searched for his second intercostal space. In the mid-clavicular line, he lined up the cannula just above the third rib so as to avoid the nerve bundle which ran along the bottom of the ribs, and pushed. He heard a hiss of air. And almost immediately the gunner began to respond. He had relieved the tension pneumothorax, and turned it into a simple pneumothorax, which would need to be drained-but not so urgently. But Ian also knew that the cannula was only a temporary solution- it might kink and then the tension would start once more. He needed to get him to good medical aid fast. But for now the pressure was off. He had bought himself some time.

But then all of this became immaterial. For very suddenly Ian was surrounded. Male voices screamed at him in Arabic. And he was being hit, and kicked. And he tensed against the hits, wondering where his pistol was and why had he not drawn it and fired- but it was too late to do anything for their kicks were too strong, and they had taken his pistol and pulled away his shotgun and now both were against his head. And then a bag had been put over his head, and his hands were tied tight behind his back. And he was lifted by two men from under his arms, and he was forced to run. And he could not see where he was going, and he kept tripping, and shivering and trembling. And he had been thrown into the back of a truck, and was being sat on, and men whispered to each other in Arabic- and the engine had been turned on, and all was dark around him, and the doors were shut- and the truck began to drive. And then the first kidnapper said to him in a dense Arabic accent, "welcome to your end infidel. Allahu Akhbar. Allahu Akhbar. Allahu Akhbar!"

Chapter Fifteen: Paralysis

Ian was eventually pulled out of the car, and taken into a building. He still knew nothing of where he was. He could see nothing. Voices were all around him, and they laughed at him, and they prodded him, and they hit him. After sometime of trying to plead with them, he realised it was best to keep his mouth shut- for whenever he spoke he was hit. After perhaps half an hour of this (it was difficult to keep track of time), he was thrown onto the floor of an empty room and a door was bolted behind him. He physically shook with fear, terrified of what was to happen to him. He knew what terrorists did with prisoners. He gulped. He waited second by second for someone to come in and kill him, to beat him, to cut him or to shoot him. His shivers were all there was to remind him of his being alive. And as he shivered he cursed the secret service, and everything else to do with it. And he cursed himself for joining it for being so stupid. So greedy and so stupid. And here he was left for what seemed like an age. Would they torture him? He could not say anything? But what did he know to say? He had been given no secrets

He could only tell from under the bag over his head, which itched and irritated his skin, that he remained in the room over two long and terrible nights. He was given small amounts of rice and water, but whenever he was given these the bag was very strictly pulled up from his mouth, and his eyes still covered over blocking his sight. Now and then someone would enter to shout at or hit him. He tried to sit against the wall and get sleep, but every time he drifted off- he would be woken by noises, or his own rank fear. He prayed for the first time in years. He prayed that Merlin would have some plan to find him- that he would have some secret tracker device on Ian and soon he would burst in and save the day with a diagnosis. But as the hours had turned to days, Ian realised that no one was coming for him. He was alone.

When Ian had begun to lose hope of ever getting out of this mess alive, two men came into the room and lifted him up. They took him into a car, and then drove him somewhere. They had lowered their voices, it seemed they did not want to be discovered. Ian's trembles had stopped as he had come to accept his surroundings. Every now and then they hit him, and eventually they took him into what seemed to be someone's house. He could hear a TV, or a radio.

Bruised and battered they threw Ian into a room. He fell to the floor. Bent double on all fours, someone removed his blind fold. His eyes tensed in pain, he had not seen light for some time. He shivered uncontrollably. The carpet was dark brown, and old. It smelt of must. "You are doctor- my father, he is sick- help him now- help him now!" Someone hit Ian on the back of the head. Rubbing it, he looked up. He was in a small living room. A TV played an Arabic game show, and he made out an elderly man in an arm chair. "Help him!" The man pointed.

"Okay, Okay!" Ian retorted sluggishly, not entirely sure who he was supposed to help and why. He shook himself to try to snap out of the sleep deprived state he was in. A man with a shemagh covering his head grabbed his arm and pulled him up over to the man in the chair. The man bent forward and lifted the man's right arm, which flopped down immediately. The man also prodded at his cheek, which was hanging lower than the left. The man simply sat gazing forward into nothingness. He was drooling from his right lip, which did not seem to close properly. "Help him!" The man shouted again. He said something to the other man present in Arabic, who made a sound of agreement. Ian bent over and tried to clear his mind. What was this?

"Hello sir? Sir?" He mumbled.

"What is wrong with him?" The man wearing the scarf ejected.

"Hello sir?" Ian looked at his face, and general right side of the body. It had marked decreased tone. The elderly man tried to speak, but his speech was slurred and pathetic. This looked like a stroke. After some time he stared straight ahead again, apathic.

"I need my medical bag. Where is my medical bag?" Ian asked the man confidently. Being able to understand the workings of this man's illness more than his kidnappers made him no longer feel so inferior and gave him some comfort. The man went out of the room and threw a bag at him. It was his bag, at least he could be thankful they had that- perhaps he could look more like he was helping this man with it. He went through A, B, C's. The man was in Atrial Fibrillation, a risk factor Ian knew for cerebral infarct. But really Ian would have to take a CT scan or MRI of the man's head to rule out a haemorrhage before administering any thrombolysis. The man hit him on the back of the head again, this time harder than the other times. What should he do? Would they kill him if he did nothing? If it had been more than 4 hours since the onset of symptoms, the treatments would be ineffective.

"When did this happen?" Ian asked instinctively.

"Sudden, sudden! Yesterday! You do something, you fix him!" Ian knew that neurological symptoms resulting from cerebrovascular diseases are sudden in onset. Only very occasionally would other neurological diagnoses present suddenly such as brain tumours, demyelination (multiple sclerosis) and hypoglycaemia. If these symptoms had started yesterday, there was little in the way thrombolysis could do. Ian could also rule out a Transient Ischaemic Attack or TIA, for the symptoms would have resolved within 24 hours. Ian needed to work out what area of the brain had been affected by the stroke, for this would affect the man's prognosis. Perhaps a carotid artery ultrasound might have been a good option for the man, but Ian was never going to be able to do one of those, even if he had the equipment. What was he going to do? He needed to show them he was treating him. The man hit him on his shoulder blade with the butt of his machine gun. Ian fell to the floor in agony. The pain was intense. "You will fix him now or we will kill you! We will cut off your head like a pig! A pig!"

Whether it was adrenaline that kept Ian calm at hearing this, he did not know, but he did not break down. He focused on how he was going to help the man. Maybe administering prophylaxis might be a good way to show he was treating him? He had the drugs in his bag… Whatever he did, he had to do it now.

"Right. I need to do some tests on him." He stood up confidently. He felt on the cliff edge of life and death, and knew that in order to keep himself from falling off his mind would have to remain clear. He asked himself where the brain lesion was.

"Tell him to relax. I am going to feel his limbs." He inspected both upper and lower limbs for wasting, scarring and fasiculations. He felt for tone, moving the arms and legs in turn. The right side had markedly increased tone. He tested for power. "Can you put your arms out like a chicken impression?!" He said in English. "Ask him to do this." He turned to the man and showed the action he wanted the man to copy. After some Arabic, the man was not able to lift his right arm, but the left raised fine. "Tell him to push against me with both arms!" Eventually the man cooperated, and Ian assessed that his power on the left was 5/5 on the MRC scale, and on the right it was 1/5.

"Tap your right hand onto your left and flip it over repeatedly- as fast as you can." Ian wanted to test for Dysdiodikinesia and coordination. Trying to get this conveyed was hopeless though- they did not understand, so he gave up after a few minutes. "Get him to touch his nose with his right hand's index finger and then touch my finger." Eventually this worked, and there was no past pointing or signs of ataxia. He tested for signs of Hemiballismus, Nystagmus and Intention tremor/inattention of which he could not elicit any. It was difficult though, he seemed to have a homonymous heminanopia which may have mimicked the inattention. He ruled out a cerebellar stroke, and after performing a quick sensory test which revealed lessened sensation over the right side, he ruled out a Lacunar infarct (LACS) which generally showed a purely motor defecit.

Ian made a guess that this was a TACS or total anterior circulation stroke, as there was higher cerebral function defecits (there seemed to be expressive and receptive dysphasia), a dense Hemiplegia and a hemianopia. A partial anterior circulation stroke or PACS would have only shown two of those three findings, and a POCS or posterior circulation stroke would have shown brain stem symptoms of which Ian could see none. But what did this matter? What could he do for the man? He had had a big stroke.

"Help him now! Now! GIVE HIM MEDICINE!" The man cocked his weapon.

"No! No! Don't shoot! Please!" Begging, Ian rustled frantically in his medical bag. He would treat him as if he had had a stroke within the last 4 hours. He had no other option, the kidnappers were more and more edgy. He knew this would do nothing for him but thought it might buy him some time at least. Really the man needed to be admitted to a stroke ward and have aggressive physiotherapy, DVT prophylaxis by perhaps heparin, NG feeding and rehabilitation- after investigations for risks of another cerebral event.

But this was not the time to be thinking of rehabilitation. Ian was in a very dark corner of his life, and at the moment he saw no way out of it. But giving the man some medication and making it look like he was doing something, appease them? He fumbled around and eventually pulled out the aspirin from his bag. The men grew more impatient, pacing around him and breathing down his neck. He looked at it hard. He tried to remember the dose Merlin had told him so long ago. His hand was trembling and he fought to steady it. He did not want to appear scared, maybe they would think him incompetent. But what if it had been a haemorrhage? Could he be sure it was an infarction and not a bleed? "Help him now! NOW!" They hit him to the floor. And they continued to hit him.

Many times they hit him and Ian waited for it to stop. But it did not stop. Ian had dropped the Aspirin and the tablets had fallen everywhere. They kicked him now. This was it, Ian thought. Time for his life to come to an end. He thought of his family, and of his mother. What would they tell her? "I will cut your head off like a pig!" The man shouted, and still the other one kicked him. One man had gone to get his knife, and Ian had given in to nothingness now for what could he do but die? Blood coming from many wounds on him, battered, bruised and bloody nosed he struggled to even tense against the blows. His vision blurred. Still he could hear them shouting at him. Still he could hear their terrifying screams.

Through the ringing ears and the pain- there was an almighty crash. The kicks and hitting stopped. Bangs and booms of gunfire and grenades, and bullets hitting flesh filled the house, smoke and flashes and confusion and choking and blood. Men had run into the room and were shouting things, but Ian was dazed, he did not understand- there were more Arabic voices? Was he to get shot? Was he being kidnapped again? A body landed on top of him- blood poured from its neck. Ian turned it over. It was one of the men who had hit him. He pushed it away as if he was on fire. But Ian still had not given the aspirin to the elderly man, he needed to give it to him to survive. He frantically finger picked at the aspirin tablets scattered on the floor, desperate.

But someone grabbed him and lifted him up- they put another bag over his head- they shouted at him in Arabic- and English, someone in the room was definitely speaking English- but Ian did not care for just before the bag had been put over his head he saw something which sapped all hope in him that there was even an ounce of goodness in the world. It had all been in vain. Amongst the smoke and the crashes and the bangs and the booms- the elderly man whom he had just diagnosed as having a TAC stroke, had bullet holes through his head, his chest and his legs and he was no more.

So helplessness took Ian and he began to cry like a lost child. Crying, shaking, and sobbing pathetically, he was manhandled out of the house and into the back of another jeep. And off he was driven yet again to a location he did not know.

Chapter Sixteen: Merlin's Surprise

The vehicle rumbled loudly, swaying left and right as they ripped around corners. Ian was sat in between people. The cool metal barrel of a rifle rested against his leg. Could he grab it? He was done for now anyway. He did not care what would happen to him. Could he grab it? Arabic voices over the sound of the engine. A familiar voice, "Ian! Ian! Ian!" The bag was pulled off his head.

Ian did not at first look into Maljef's eyes. He thought it best not to offend his kidnappers. "Dr Ian, Dr Ian! Are you okay? Dr Ian!" Maljef shouted from the front seat staring back. "We take you to safety now Dr Ian!" Ian looked up and stared into Maljef's brown eyes. It took him several moments to realise who it was. Then, on realising he was no longer in enemy hands he burst into tears again, this time with relief. He took Maljef's hand, and would not let go of it. "Thank you, thank you, thank you, thank you," he repeated. For the first time since Ian's father had died all those years ago, he prayed.

"It's okay, we find you, we find you sir! We take you to your people now!" Ian shook hands with the men next to him, again and again, and he patted the driver on the back. They followed another vehicle, full of other Iraqi men who helped free him. He wished he could jump out and kiss them.

After several hours of driving, they arrived at a heavily guarded compound, surrounded by electric fences and cornered off by concrete bunkers. "We arrive." Maljef said, helping him out of the jeep. Ian clambered clumsily out. His legs creaked with stiffness. The heat hit him, and he hobbled after Maljef who took him towards a concrete building. Before he reached it, out of the door came a familiar face. Merlin smiled at Ian, and patted him on the arm. It took Ian a moment to recognise him. Like seeing a person you are used to seeing in a certain environment, in a totally different environment- it did not make sense.

"Ian how are you? Slight blip in your flight plan I understand," he smiled and patted him on the back. Ian stood still and stared at him. He clenched his fist tightly with fury.

"What are you doing here? Haven't you done enough?" he said bitterly.

"Sorry? You got caught up in war unfortunately. This is just the way it goes sometimes."

"The way it goes? The way it goes! For the last days I thought I was going to be beheaded- I have been beaten! And all you say is its unfortunate? I was kidnapped and all you can say is that is the way things go sometimes!"

"I can see you are angry. Good. I will speak to you when you have calmed down," Merlin turned to walk away.

"No you won't! Get me straight back to England I have had enough of this mess- this stupid excuse for a job!"

"Take some time to rest, you need to be declared medically fit anyway," Merlin said, turning abruptly on the spot. He began to walk away into the building. Ian's eyes were bursting out of their sockets. Captain Jim Reece grabbed Ian by the arm, and gently led him away into a medical room of some sort.

"Have a few hours kip Ian, and let Corporal Williams here tend to your wounds. Glad you are back safe and sound, you had me worried there." Ian did not reply, but lay down on the lady corporal's command on the bed. She began to dress his cuts and clean his face. "I must ask you Ian, did you tell them anything about our organisation? This is very important." Jim said seriously.

"No! There was not a chance to even if I had wanted."

"Ok. Ok. Well done lad," Jim continued to talk to him about what had happened, and how it had happened, but Ian, overwhelmed with freedom, with agony and with tiredness, fell asleep in an instant.

Ian slept deeply overnight and dreamt of being in a coffee shop with a waitress called Kate. But unfortunately he awoke to an empty room, and a bright harsh sun rising over a vast desert. He felt better for the rest. He gathered his thoughts. He was safe. Thank god! He still could not believe the gargantuan mess up that had just occurred. But alas it was over. It was all over. The cuts and bruises he had gained stung more this morning.

He had breakfast, and felt stronger. Following his ration of toast, bacon and eggs he had a visitor. Merlin stood at the end of his bed. He was more subdued than normal, but was not taking any nonsense. "So, you still want to give up? Give up at this last hurdle?"

"Give up? Give up! Do you not know what I have just been through?" Ian seethed, on the verge of screaming. Merlin stared at him. He shook his head slowly like a disappointed headmaster in a pupil they thought would go far. His eyes rolled. Despite Ian's state, it struck deep into his heart. Recent capture and beatings aside, a surge of excitement came upon Ian. He was so close. Was he really going to let it escape him? He knew this was going to be difficult. "There is really only one more step?"

"I will not argue with you Mellows. You have to want to get into the secret service and become a secret doctor- you have to want it. Otherwise, we would not be the best in the world- which we are. You have to want it a lot. Our members have gone through far worse over our history, do not think you are an exception. If you are willing to have a tantrum when things go wrong- then frankly we do not want you. Do not dare to think you have gone through more than others. Do not dare," he began to walk away.

"Wait," Ian said. Merlin turned impatiently.

"Stop messing me around Ian. Do you want me to tell you about your final exam or not?"

"Yes. Ok. I do want to continue," Ian said after a brief moment of thought. It was too much to simply throw away. How would he go back to normal medical school after this? He just wanted to sleep, but sleep could come later.

"Good. 10:00 in the briefing room and I will explain. And do not dare patronise me and tell me I do not know what you have gone through. Just as I know nothing of your last experience- you know nothing of what I have gone through in my life. Never presume you know better than someone else," he paused. Ian felt embarrassed for he was right. Some welcome back to freedom this was. Merlin trudged out of the building without saying another word, leaving Ian blushing. Merlin did have a knack for making people blush.

Chapter Seventeen: Last Test

Merlin was briefing Ian in the other room, and Jim got everything prepared. Jim loaded rounds into the magazine of his pistol and placed them away into his assault vest. He had checked through the medical kit on the chopper, but he was uneasy. Merlin entered. "Right, he knows what he needs to do. You happy?"

"No, not really Klaus." Jim answered scratching his forehead. "If you want my opinion I think he is still very fragile. Too fragile. This is not just one your normal tests- this is a warzone."

"Don't you think both he and I know that? He has just been in that warzone for the past few days for god's sake! He knows the risks. But this is what this organisation is all about. Queen and country. Going the extra mile- pushing through to the last. This way I can be totally sure he is suitable."

"But this is dangerous- too dangerous Klaus! Look what happened last time! You and I both know we nearly lost him- those terrorists were going to televise his execution!"

"Do you not think *your* final exam was as dangerous as this? Do you not remember that- the state you were in, Jim?"

"I remember it as if it were yesterday," Jim retorted agitatedly. He thought of Miss Adbajal. "But I had not just been captured and beaten!"

"The jungles of the Congo were beating enough. Ian gets this out of the way quicker. You were in that rebel hospital for eight weeks. If there were a way to measure being deprived- I bet you would not have scored so differently to what Ian is now."

Jim paused. Merlin was probably right. It was easy to forget one's achievements. He was being soft on Mellows. "Fine. You are right." he finally stated.

"Of course I am right. I have not instated nigh on forty medical students into our ranks to not be right," he sat down. "Anyhow- it is simple enough, a casualty evacuation- he manages a patient correctly and without flapping, and he passes. I'll be on the chopper to make sure it goes well. Not that he will know that."

Jim carried on loading his pistol. They were on call now to go out with the medical emergency response team for the next 12 hours. He wondered when they would get the call. Ian walked into the room, as Merlin was leaving. "Good luck boy- I'll be on the radio set in case you need me. Remember, this is about you keeping your cool and being safe- not about you knowing the exact ins and outs of treatment." Ian nodded. Merlin left, and Ian sat next to Jim.

"What if I get captured again?" he said fearfully. Jim felt bad for him. What an ordeal he had been through. But then, this organisation was not for just anyone.

"Just follow your principles- keep your head down, and when it is over- the world is your oyster." Ian smiled.

"True," he retorted.

They sat in silence for some time, Ian wiping some of the cuts he had been given by his kidnappers, and rubbing his bruises. Jim noticed that Ian kept checking and re-checking his morphine stock. They sat in the room for a couple of hours, and in the middle of a conversation about their favourite types of Sunday roast, the red telephone rang. Jim answered immediately. Ian sat up and put his body armour on. This was it.

"MERT, Captain Reece speaking. Yes. Yes. Yes. Roger that, moving to you," he paused scribbling notes into his notepad. Ian looked at him, Jim thought he looked terrified. He probably was. "Right come on. An infantry patrol has hit an IED. Two casualties. This is it. Remember CABCs- you'll be fine mate."

They walked out and headed to the helipad. Jim looked at Ian and felt proud- he could see the difference in the boy that he trained only a matter of months ago. This boy had become a man. The Chinook's engine was already blearing, the rotary blades spinning. Ian did not notice Merlin sitting up front with the pilot. Before they knew what was happening, they had taken off.

Jim looked over at Ian as they drew nearer to the destination. At least there was not incoming enemy fire on the ground- it would relieve some of the stress for Ian. The chopper drew to a standstill in the air, and then began to sink lower and lower towards Iraq's harsh desert soil. Jim smiled at Ian, and Ian smiled back looking terrified. He would be ok though, Jim knew it.

They touched down and the Chinook jolted. The exit ramp slowly opened. A widening beam of sunlight shone in from Iraq's harsh sun. Jim moved to the rear of the helicopter, and then the gunfire started. Jim relayed orders over the radio set. Should they take off now? No- they could get the casualties in. George the patrol medic met him at the Chinook entrance. He took him over to the casualties. There were three. Ian could manage this. He darted back to the Chinook amongst bullets whizzing around- and found Ian cowering in the helicopter. He looked pathetic. Some healthy encouragement, and he grabbed him and threw him out of the helicopter. They ran back over to the casualties. Ian simply stared, dumbstruck at them. He needed more guidance than Jim had hoped. "You'll have to take care of that one on your own or they'll both die!" he shouted. Ian looked sharp, got on his radio set to Merlin, and Jim started with George on the casualty in front of him. The poor lad was in a bad way. T1 was written on his forehead- an urgent priority. Both his legs were blown off, and he was badly burnt. He started at first principles, being careful to bear in mind the treatment of the acute burns patient. The bleeding looked to be controlled by two Combat Application Torniquets over each thigh. But he wondered what the chance of him surviving was.

The burns would cause progressive cell death if the temperatures were high. Burns led to increased capillary permeability and loss of fluid from the intravascular space. Jim had to be very aware of Systemic Inflammatory Response Syndrome developing, a progressive process that continues to develop for several hours after the burn. Toxins released from the burn wound stimulate SIRS, and can overwhelm patients and lead to death. He needed to urgently get fluids into the man, but he was weary as too much fluid can result in excessive oedema in burns victims. He was getting carried away. He looked to first principles. CABCDEs. Catastrophic haemorrhage was dealt with just about. Airway- He had to be aware of an inhalation injury caused by inhalation of hot gases from flame, smoke or steam. A huge explosion nearby made Jim duck over the patient and they were covered in earth and sand.

Jim shook himself and carried on. He thought he should be aware of inhalation problems, but he had some time. It was an open area in which the burn had happened. The airway seemed patent. He was aware that airway can become obstructed due to oedema and swelling so mentally thought about where his surgical intubation kit was. For now though, he needed to perform rapid sequence induction anaesthesia and intubate this patient early. An explosion boomed in the distance. The gunner roared on the 50 cal. Machine gun.

He moved onto Breathing. Fast and shallow. But seemed ok for now. He was aware burns could lead to pulmonary failure over 24 hours depending on the fumes inhaled. He could worry about that later. He gave 100% oxygen through a non-re-breathe mask in case of carbon monoxide poisoning. Bullets whizzed overhead.

He moved on to Circulation. He got the two wide bore cannulas in through the burns, and started wondering about administering extra fluids through an interosseous needle into the bone. He started a bag of Hartmanns. Burns patients lost fluids very rapidly due to the loss of skin integrity. He also knew that full thickness burns can obstruct the blood supply to limbs due to the oedema which effectively makes a tourniquet around a limb. He thought this was the case on the patient's right arm, and went about performing an escharotomy- an incision through the scar tissue to relieve the pressure. He needed to get this patient to help soon- escharotomies could bleed terribly.

He went about trying to assess the level of the burns. The rule of nines saw that various areas of the body made up 9% of total body surface area, where the front or back of a patient's limb, for example, made up 9% of their total body surface area. He could not work this out in the heat of the battle and used the palms of his hand. Roughly one patients palm equalled 1% of burn. He also needed to assess the level of the burns, as in how deep they had gone. There were three categories- full thickness, partial thickness and superficial.

But before he could- he noticed the patient's conscious level was going down and down. Then another explosion boomed. They were sprayed with shards of shrapnel- one lodged in Jim's body armour. Suddenly George was thrown to the floor. Blood pumped from his neck and a hole in his chest. Shit. "Get me the thoracotomy set!" Jim shouted at Ian, who had managed his casualty well.

He went about CABCDEs for George now. His principles of triage were going out of the window and he knew it. It was all going out of the window. He had to get them out of there. He looked over to see Ian sprinting towards him, but then he heard another explosion, and a bullet had ripped right through Ian's leg and it had almost taken the foot off. He was on the dust now too. He sprinted to Ian and got a tourniquet on above the wound. "It'll be ok mate! Ian! Ian!" He ran back to cover and radioed for Merlin, he needed extra help. It did not matter the man was almost ninety. They were desperate. Jim went about dealing with George, but there was no use. He was dead. The burnt casualty, was also dead, oxygen hissed out through the mask over a lifeless face.

Crouching behind the wall, Jim watched as Merlin ran over to Ian to start treating him. They had to get out of there. He made the decision to leave George and the burnt soldier. There was nothing more he could do. He went to help Merlin.

Ian was unconscious. He had lost a lot of blood. The tourniquet around his leg was holding. They would scoop and run, frantically pulling Ian towards the Chinook amongst gunfire. Merlin stood up to straighten his back- and that was when it happened. Whoosh! A bullet ripped right into him, just where his kidney was. Blood spurted out- it had certainly hit an artery and god knows what else. Merlin fell forward onto Jim. Jim rushed with him into the Chinook. He sat on the edge of the ramp, and saw

Ian lying out in the middle of the chaos- bullets and tracer rounds and grenades bursting all around. He almost said to the pilot to leave before he went back for him. He felt ashamed about that for some time afterwards. But he did not. With one last bound of energy, he ran back and pulled Ian into the back of the Chinook ordering the other men to get Merlin and Ian's casualty ready for transport. The ambush response team helped him in. He saw one of the enemy running towards them, but the gunner shot them both. It was all a big mess.

Captain Jim Reece now had a dilemma. He had two serious casualties to treat, one very young, one very old. Both of whom he knew. But he could not bring himself to triage one over the other. Merlin was losing a lot of blood and deteriorating rapidly. There was no way to get a tourniquet onto the area.

Gradually, Merlin began to tire and he became more and more unresponsive. And he smiled at Jim, and then he said, "Take care of Mellows- it's about time I went." Jim held his hand, smiled and gave him some more morphine. Merlin closed his eyes slowly, as if about to drift off to sleep. Jim moved onto Ian with tears in his eyes. Ian was pretty well sedated now to alleviate the pain. Booms and bangs were now underneath them- and they were flying back to the main hospital. He hoped to

God they would not both die. There were more doctors there. They would help.

Chapter Eighteen: Darkness

Ian did not know if he was asleep. He did not know if he was awake. He did not know if he was alive. He did not know if he was dead. In fact, he did not know anything in his current state. He did not even know enough to be able to wonder if he was asleep, or if he was awake, or if he was alive, or if he was dead. All he knew was darkness. And even the darkness he did not really know. He did not know pain. He did not know fear. He did not know whether he was real. He knew nothing. But in knowing nothing, he began to strain to know something.

Into the darkness came a sharp feeling at the back of his throat. And something intruded into his unconsciousness of a pain. And then another intrusion of a voice. And then someone rubbing his leg. And then he thought he might have vomited in the blackness. But then it was darkness again. Simple, unfailing, unchallenged, dark, black, darkness. His ears whistled briefly. But then the darkness came over him again. The sound of a helicopter. And then more, unending darkness.

Gradually, as these interruptions came into his dark, black and unconscious world, he began to realise he was alive. And even though he could not identify with anything in the present, it made him happy. The odd interruption of a voice which sounded like Dr Merlin's, or an emotion for the hated Mr Bing, or the worry that he would fail his exams, or the missing of home, or the general feeling of being alive, came into his dark world. But Ian could not piece together these emotions, for unconsciousness still gripped him more than consciousness.

He strained for consciousness, even though he knew not what consciousness was. And as the anaesthetist began to bring him round letting him breath more O2, an interruption different from the others came to him. Whether this was a dream, whether it was reality or whether it was neither of the two, Ian did not know. Nor did he care. He had no care in the world, nor did he have a world to have a care in. And in this nothingness he was. And then an emotion gripped him. And then he felt pain. And then, he woke up.

The military hospital was blurry. He was hazy from the anaesthetic. His eyes strained to focus. He heard noises around him. He saw a figure in front of him. "Merlin? Merlin?"

Mr Vesely leant over the bed and touched his shoulder, "Wake up Ian, wake up my lad."

"Merlin? Did I pass? Did I pass!"

"This is Mr Vesely Ian. Mr Vesely!" Ian's eyes focused more after some moments. He identified Vesely and Jim. Why was Vesely in the room?

"Jim?"

"Yes I am here Ian. I am here," he looked at the ground. "What are you doing here Mr Vesely?"

"I'm here to give you some news."

"Yes?" He looked at him like an innocent child.

"Dr Merlin is dead Ian." Ian felt a sharp pain going through his leg, and another pain which no amount of morphine nor any pain killer would cure. He winced.

"Dead?"

Jim explained how it had happened. He explained how Merlin, had pretty much saved his life. Ian was gutted. And amongst the sadness and deep deep mourning of Merlin, he felt relieved. But then, he was confused. Why was he here?

"I will be taking Dr Merlin's place now Ian."

"Sorry?"

"I was next in line to head the secret doctor's."

"Mr Vesely?"

"You can cut the Mr Vesely Ian, my name is Martin," he paused. "My first duty will be to instate a medical student into the secret service who has satisfied our training demands. Congratulations, Ian Mellows, you have passed," he shook Ian's hand, and placed a degree certificate on his bedside table. "Congratulations Doctor Mellows. Welcome to the club."

THE END

Printed in Great Britain
by Amazon